RAIDERS OF THE VALLEY

RAIDERS OF THE VALLEY

Tom Curry

CHIVERS
THORNDIKE

This Large Print book is published by BBC Audiobooks Ltd, Bath, England and by Thorndike Press®, Waterville, Maine, USA.

Published in 2005 in the U.K. by arrangement with Golden West Literary Agency.

Published in 2005 in the U.S. by arrangement with Golden West Literary Agency.

U.K. Hardcover   ISBN 1–4056–3168–6 (Chivers Large Print)
U.K. Softcover   ISBN 1–4056–3169–4 (Camden Large Print)
U.S. Softcover   ISBN 0–7862–7032–2 (Nightingale)

The text of this Large Print edition is unabridged.

Other aspects of the book may vary from the original edition.

Set in 16 pt. New Times Roman.

Printed in Great Britain on acid-free paper.

British Library Cataloguing in Publication Data available

Library of Congress Control Number: 2004111179

CHAPTER ONE

RAID

Felipe Castro was so astounded by what he had heard Manfred von Wohl say that he did not grow angry for moments.

'This note is for twenty thousand dollars, Castro, not for two thousand as you seem to think,' von Wohl had just said.

'But yuh mak' meestake, Senor von Wohl,' Castro protested earnestly. 'You see, I borrow two thousand dollars only. You bought ze note, *si*, but now eet's paid. In your hand ees the mon-ees.'

Von Wohl was a cold-faced man, a Prussian transplanted to the great West of the United States—where he did not belong. He had a square, strong body, and stiff flaxen hair which he kept short-clipped as he did his bristling mustache of which he was inordinately vain. A whitish scar from a Heidelberg student's saber cut diagonally from his left eye corner to his brutish chin. It was a cut which had healed poorly, so that scar tissue stood out prominently against the tan of his flat cheek. His somewhat protuberant, light blue eyes were cruelly cold.

Felipe Castro knew little of the German, who had recently come to dwell in the valley of

1

the Salinas River, south of old Monterey. Castro, a ranchero, was a product of the golden days of his people, the Americans of Spanish stock who had settled southern California on the heels of Padre Junipero Serra and other brave priests who had built their missions in the wilderness and worked against great odds to convert and teach the Indians.

These gracious, open-hearted folks, who were Castro's people, had come from Mexico, and had taken naturally to cattle and horse raising. Great ranchos had spread along the fertile Salinas Valley, touching that strange river called 'upside-down' because it ran the wrong way, from south to north. The Santa Lucia range, rugged and steep, and only twenty-five miles to the west, cut off the valley from the Pacific Coast.

But the heyday of such huge ranches was over. Shrewd men had come from the East and from Europe. They were better at business than the rancheros and some were tricky, even dishonest. The prodigal hospitality, the chests filled with money, uncounted because there was always more than enough, the easy, gracious, sunny life, all these were going.

Felipe Castro was a polished gentleman who had been born to the land. His chief hope was to be able to leave at least some of his fast disappearing wealth to his sons, Pastor and Ygnacio.

2

Slim in body, his graceful form set off by dark velvet trousers and jacket, and with hair and goatee grayed by the years, Castro now faced the powerful von Wohl who threatened that remaining hope.

It was hard for Castro, the soul of honesty, whose word was his bond, to comprehend such rascality.

*   *   *

Two years before, during the terrible drought, he had borrowed two thousand dollars. He had just paid it to von Wohl, who had purchased the note, and Castro had asked for the return of the note, but the Prussian would not give him the legal paper.

'See for yourself,' said von Wohl, holding it up so that Castro could read the figures. 'The amount of this is twenty thousand dollars, Castro. I want it now, today, or I want a quit-claim deed to your ranch. You know I can take you to court and make a lot of trouble. All your other creditors will close in on you when they hear I'm suing you, and it will only cost you more money to fight me.'

Castro drew himself up.

'Either you or some other thief has raised the amount on the note, Senor von Wohl,' he accused. 'Now I want you to get out. You refuse to give me the note or the money you have tricked me into paying, for I would not have given you the two thousand if I had known what you meant to do. No gentleman would act as you have.'

The heat of blood in his veins made Castro's head throb. He was infuriated, as he ordered von Wohl off. He was not afraid, even of the huge, bullet-headed fellow who backed von Wohl—'Hans,' he was called.

Von Wohl spoke to this Hans in the tone of a superior as he gave quick orders. Outside the wide doorway a dozen tough-faced, armed men sat their horses, watching. They also had come with von Wohl.

Von Wohl did not budge; his chin stuck out, and his head was thrown back, exposing his bull neck.

'You're a fool, Castro,' he declared. 'An old fool who's way behind the times. I don't like your sort. You jackass, I've given you fair warning.'

He took a threatening step toward Castro, scowling ferociously. Castro stood his ground.

Suddenly von Wohl slapped Castro in the face. No man could brook such an insult and, with a sharp cry, Castro dropped a hand to his knife, either to draw it and fight or to threaten and drive von Wohl out.

It was enough of an excuse for von Wohl. As the giant Hans leaped forward to help the man who so plainly was his master, von Wohl whipped a pistol and fired into the ranchero's body. Castro crumpled on the mat.

4

'*Gut* shot, Herr von Wohl,' Hans said. He knelt to check Castro. 'He iss dead, sir.'

Hans showed the utmost servility toward von Wohl. There was doglike devotion in his small green eyes as he addressed his chief. Hans had been a private in the Prussian army, while von Wohl had been an officer. The gap between such was not to be bridged.

Von Wohl's neck now was brick-red in his fighting rage. He gnawed at his crisp mustache. He had not spoken when two young men, alarmed by the cracking shot, came running through from another room. They were nice-looking boys, in their late teens— Pastor and Ygnacio, Felipe's sons. They saw the still figure on the floor, saw the life blood draining away.

'You have killed my father!' the elder of the two, Pastor, cried.

Von Wohl was glaring at them, and the gorilla-like Hans turned to frown on them. Hans could be a frightening figure, even without a frown. He weighed over three hundred pounds but did not seem overweight, his frame was so large. He had a shaven, bullet head, small greenish eyes, a hooked nose, and hands that were enormous even for such a big fellow.

Von Wohl still held the smoking pistol as he swung on the boys. They were armed, carrying knives and revolvers, as did most of the vaqueros and riders of the Salinas.

'Hold them, Hans!' snapped von Wohl.

*   *   *

Pastor and Ygnacio saw von Wohl's gun covering them. Pastor gave a sharp cry, dropping to his knee as he drew his pistol to defend himself and his brother. Von Wohl's shot missed, and Pastor fired at him across the wide living room.

Von Wohl, startled at the closeness of the bullet past his head, leaped for the cover afforded by a thick chest near at hand, yelling for his men. The riders jumped off their horses and rushed toward the door, shotguns and Colts ready.

Swiftly the young Castros ran back through the house. A woman, somewhere, was screaming at the commotion. Von Wohl sent a hasty slug after the Castro brothers, and Pastor staggered, his arm spurting blood. Ygnacio threw an arm about his brother and jumped with him through a door, which took them out of von Wohl's sight.

'After 'em—shoot the fools down!' roared von Wohl. His gang surged through the hacienda, pounding after the young fellows who had pelted out a back way and were mounting sleek long-limbed horses. The shrieking woman, gunshots, and the curses of bloodthirsty killers disturbed the balmy, gentle air of the Salinas afternoon.

CHAPTER TWO

TO THE RESCUE

Now and then David Kenny, who had paused for a rest on a knoll above the Castro rancho, would pat the small bulge his money made in the leather wallet secured under his blue shirt. He took comfort from the feel of it, in the assurance that it was still there.

He had earned it by hardships, pain, and toil. Most of it had been saved out of his pay as a drummer boy and soldier in the late conflict between North and South, the awful Civil War. With the money were papers of which he was proud—his honorable discharge from the Army, a commendation for bravery in the face of enemy fire.

The war had seared its horrors deep in Kenny's young mind. He had been wounded in the leg near the end of the fighting, as Grant had pushed Lee into the trap from which there was no escape. It had taken nearly a year for the leg to heal, though good health and his youth had finally done it.

Kenny had gone back home to the little Pennsylvania town from which he had been conscripted, but his mother had recently died, and there was nothing to hold him. He was restless, and he had heard there was good land in the West, to be given to discharged veterans. So he had worked his way across the great continent. It was the only way he could have reached the far-off coast, because only recently had the Union Pacific joined with Leland Stanford's Central Pacific at Ogden, Utah, to span the vast continent. It was a world-shaking junction, the joining of East and West, for at last the United States was really united.

General Grant, victor in the Civil War, was now in the White House. He also had urged that the West offered treasures and wealth to veterans who would work for it. There was gold everywhere, and opportunities in numbers for men in the growing young giant which was called America.

Of Scottish blood, David Kenny was thrifty and he had a level head. His hair was thick and light, and his face was pleasant, though his blue eyes were somber for a man so young. He still carried a reminder of his leg wound—a faint limp. Otherwise his well-knit, broad-shouldered body was in splendid physical condition.

After having ridden or walked across the continent to reach California, for a time he had worked in the placer mines around Sacramento. But the hunt for gold was so ephemeral, so many lost out, that Kenny shrewdly gave it up after a trial.

His real ambition was to become a farmer

and rancher, on a large scale. He loved all animals, especially horses and cattle, and he loved the soil. He had nearly stopped in Kansas to take up sections, but though the land was fine there for crops and herbage, the Indians were troublesome. Besides, some blind force kept driving him on, always west

He had moved south, stopped for a time in Monterey. Then he had heard of the rich Salinas Valley, and had come to see if he had at last reached the Promised Land.

Kenny was in no hurry to invest his money. He meant to look all over the territory, consider every opportunity, before making his choice. He had a good black gelding, a blanket roll for a bed, a pack containing essentials, and no ties to bind him down. Moreover, it was his habit to weigh carefully every move he made.

He was wrapped in day dreams as he sat his horse there atop the knoll, but was aroused from them by the sound of gunfire. Instantly Kenny knew what it was. He had been a soldier too long to mistake the sounds. He was on a rise covered with wild mustard, which grew in profusion where the land was not under cultivation, and he could see the winding trail along the hillsides. As he lifted his head and stared down below, he saw two horsemen on swift, fine horses who were running before a dozen more mounted men who kept firing after the pair, apparently trying desperately to hit them or their mounts.

Kenny waited. After all, the two fleeing riders might be bandits, pursued by a sheriff's posse.

As they pounded closer he could make out their vaquero clothing—short-cut jackets, tight-fitting trousers trimmed with pearl buttons. They had lost their sombreros.

One of the riders seemed in distress. He was bent over his saddle prong, while the other was trying to help him, riding close and evidently encouraging the injured one to keep going.

Kenny watched tensely as they came nearer and nearer to him, the howling gang gaining on them because one was wounded. A lucky shot—lucky for the pursuers—hit one of the beautiful horses, and nearly threw the rider. Unhurt himself, he hit the ground running, and sprang up behind his slumped companion.

'They'll never make it now!' thought Kenny, troubled lines on his bronzed brow. His nose twitched, a habit he had when trying to figure out a problem. He could see now that the two fleeing men were young, only boys. They did not look vicious, either, while the cut of many of those chasing them was tough. Kenny had been in mining and cattle camps and knew such gentry too well to err.

'I reckon I'll take a hand,' he muttered, and with Dave Kenny to decide was to act.

*   *   *

Drawing a carbine, he threw a cartridge into the breech. He sent a bullet singing over the heads of the gang. They slowed, looking in the direction of the smoke puff, to see who was interfering.

Kenny moved down to a bulge of rock which commanded the trail. When the fugitives came up he had them at his mercy, and they stared at him, the wounded man with agony in his dark eyes.

'What's goin' on?' demanded Kenny, as they paused under his steady gun.

'Senor, zey are bad hombres!' one of them cried desperately. 'Zey keel our father, Don Felipe Castro. I am Ygnacio Castro, zis ees my brother Pastor, whom they have wound. Either you help us or we die before your eyes.'

Kenny believed them. Ygnacio's words held truth.

'Hustle, then,' he said promptly. 'I'll hold 'em for you.'

'Gracias, senor,' Ygnacio said hurriedly, but fervently. 'We are going to the hacienda of our dead father's cousin, to the estate of Don Joaquin Guiterrez. Ees two mile to north of here. You weel see the buildings from the trail.'

'Ride! Go on!'

Kenny had dismounted, was crouched beside the jutting rock. He could see the killer gang clearly now. They were all rough characters, but two especially stood out. One was a huge creature with an almost bald head. Another, who was urging them on to the kill, was a square-bodied man with a bristling mustache and a scarred face.

Kenny sent another carbine bullet over them.

'Keep back, or the next'll hit home!' he called.

The whistling slug and the determination in his voice made them slow up, then stop and scatter off the trail. 'Who are you?' shouted the scar-faced man angrily. 'How dare you interfere with me?'

Peering past the jut, Kenny saw the leader signal. Several of his men dismounted and started up the slope, through the mustard. They meant to work around behind him.

It was time to move. Kenny leaped on his horse and pounded after the Castro boys.

He had slowed the killers for the minutes the Castros needed to reach the Guiterrez rancho. Kenny, snapping back at the pursuers with a soldier's trained skill, realized he had plunged into real danger. Now he needed a haven and help. His horse was lathered and bullets hummed near.

Across a dip in the beautiful land, well-grassed here, he could see where cattle grazed in bunches. The Salinas River was close at hand, in the hollow to his left. On the hill, shaded by great trees, stood a spacious hacienda, a don's home, with all the necessary barns, stables, other buildings, and corrals.

The two Castros had reached the yard. He saw them, saw that the one who had lost his horse was talking excitedly and gesticulating as he pointed first at Kenny and then at the approaching gunmen.

Kenny started down the slope, urging his horse to a final burst of speed. Von Wohl, Hans and the others whooped it up, charging after him though he did not then have an idea of their identity.

From the great rancho, vaqueros suddenly came sweeping, riding with the wonderful grace of their kind, straight at the enemy. They were led by a flashing-eyed man of middle age, with dark hair and a trimmed, black mustache. He had an air of the commander about him as he urged his men on. They were armed, yet they also held lassos in hand as they sped on, circling with wild speed, and shouting as they closed in.

Von Wohl and his men checked their charge. Then riatas began to lash out with blinding speed. Shots were hastily fired, but the vaqueros were moving fast, and von Wohl's men were being jerked off their mounts, thudding to earth, the wind knocked from them.

The leader of the vaqueros, whirling close, settled a noose over the German. Von Wohl, his gun ripped to his side as it was discharged, bellowed in helpless fury. He sailed from his

13

saddle and hit the ground.

Pastor Castro, the wounded brother, had remained at the rancho. But Ygnacio had taken his brother's horse and come out to fight. Several in von Wohl's gang had turned and ridden off in wild retreat. Others, among them von Wohl himself, were captives.

Ygnacio, fearful lest Kenny be hurt, had hurried to his side. As the quick conflict ended, Castro took Kenny to the leader of the vaqueros.

'Cousin Don Joaquin,' he said, 'here ees the man who saved our lives.'

Don Joaquin's white teeth flashed in greeting.

'I am Don Joaquin Guiterrez, senor. Everything I have ees yours. You must come weeth me.'

'My name's Dave Kenny, Don Joaquin. I didn't do much.'

*   *   *

Von Wohl, back on his feet, was glaring, mouthing threats.

'Guiterrez, you'll pay for this!'

'Shush,' snapped Guiterrez. He slapped von Wohl in the face and turned contemptuously away. 'Let the scum go, vaqueros,' he ordered. 'We are not keelers, like zem.'

Guiterrez was a slender, handsome, smiling Spanish gentleman who held his splendid head

14

high. He was gracious with Kenny, and insisted that the young man ride at his side as they returned to the rancho.

It was a king's home. Don Joaquin was a wealthy ranchero who owned thousands of horses and cattle, and the tremendous rancho. He was a fine Californian of the old school, and had held on to his property through native shrewdness and ability. Many of his peers had lost out, but so far Guiterrez had resisted the envious who sought to take his wealth.

Kenny dismounted, and a stable boy seized his horse's reins. As he turned to enter the gate, Kenny's heart leaped as he saw the girl who stood there looking at Don Joaquin and the guest he brought. She was small and exquisite, with dark hair and large eyes. She held her head with the pride of the high-bred Spanish beauty.

'Welcome!' cried Don Joaquin to Kenny as they entered the hacienda. 'You are our honored guest!'

Kenny was overwhelmed by the don's kindness. Apparently nothing was too good for the visitor. Guiterrez introduced Kenny to his wife, Donna Ysabel, and to his daughter, Teresa, the little beauty with the laughing eyes he had first seen through the gates.

With Teresa present, though demurely silent across the great room, it was difficult for Kenny to talk, to reply to Don Joaquin's queries as to himself and his experiences. The

15

Pennsylvanian was fascinated by the girl and could not help staring at her.

'Zees von Wohl, he ees a Prussian swine,' Guiterrez was saying. 'I have hear' of heem. He leeves at the Salinas crossroads, to the northwest of here, and he has man-ee hombres, tough fellows from the mines to the north.'

'Yes, senor,' said Kenny seriously. 'But I reckon we made a mistake, not killin' von Wohl off. I'm afraid he'll make plenty of trouble for you.'

It was a sobering reminder that death already had struck the peaceful Salinas land through the hand of the Prussian, von Wohl.

'I am not afraid of this cutthroat,' Don Joaquin said proudly, although his tone was not boastful. 'To live in this land a man must fight. That I have learned well.'

Kenny saw the shadow of fear cross the girl's face. He realized that she understood her father better than most. There was a good chance that Don Joaquin's hot blood could get him into a lot of danger. And von Wohl was certainly the one to make danger.

CHAPTER THREE

THE MISSION

Captain Robert Pryor, known throughout the West since the close of the Civil War as the Rio Kid, turned in his saddle and signalled his trail-mate, Celestino Mireles, the slim Mexican youth with whom he rode the danger trails of the Frontier. They had come to California on a mission, and now its beginning was in sight.

Mireles came up, guiding his gorgeous pinto with the marvelous skill of his vaquero blood. He brought the skittish gelding beside the mouse-colored dun Saber, the Rio Kid's war horse. Saber bared his wicked teeth and rippled the black stripe down his spine, but at a word from the Rio Kid he settled back his ears with a pettish toss of his head. He did not fancy other horses and would lash out at them without provocation, unless restrained.

'I reckon that's the ranch where we'll find old Jo Walker,' said the Rio Kid, indicating a low-lying building on the east slope. 'He was Kit Carson's pardner in the old days, like I told yuh. I went on a huntin' trip with Jo and Kit once, in New Mexico.'

'*Si.*' Mireles nodded. 'Walker ees great hombre, General.'

Celestino Mireles always called the Rio Kid

17

'General,' and to the young Mexican his friend and trail-mate was just that. Of course in the Civil War, the Rio Kid's title had been Captain Robert Pryor. He had been a dashing young cavalry captain in the Union Army, and had carried out the orders of Generals Grant, Sheridan and Custer with striking bravery and success. He had been a scout for the Army of the Potomac, this man from Texas, who had been forced to make the sad choice between state and country.

With the war done, though, he was the Rio Kid who rode the wild danger trails of the West, from Mexico to Canada, from the Missouri to the blue Pacific. Restless soul that he was, uprooted by the war, the Rio Kid moved from spot to spot, never tied down, always searching for adventure.

He was a handsome man, the ideal size and weight for a cavalryman, and in his blue eyes was a devil-may-care light. He clung to things reminiscent of Army days—like the blue Army shirt he wore, and the dark whipcord breeches tucked into polished, high boots, with their Army spurs. A cavalryman's campaign hat was on his head, not entirely hiding his close-cropped chestnut hair.

Crossed cartridge belts held two Colts. Another brace rode in special holsters under his shirt. His smooth cheeks were bronzed, glowing with good health. He tapered from a broad chest to the narrow waist of the fighting man.

Icy cool in the face of death, there was a commander's air about Bob Pryor. People looked to him, trusted him on sight. He had made as fine a name for himself on the Frontier as he had in the Army, and he had come to be the friend of famous men, men who could count on him when they also needed help.

Celestino Mireles was a long, lean young Mexican with a proud, hawklike visage, dark eyes, and black hair that spoke of his patrician blood. He sported Mexican clothing—the high-peaked sombrero, tight-fitting pants of his people, elegant half-boots, and a purple silk shirt. A razor-sharp knife rode beside his Colt. In the special socket attached to his saddle was a carbine, with a belt of ammunition for the rifle.

Across the Rio Grande, in old Mexico, evil men had slain Celestino's father and friends. They would have finished off Celestino, too, at the time only a lad, had not the Rio Kid come along and beaten them back.

Since that time, Mireles and the Rio Kid had been inseparable comrades, sharing the perils of the trail together, partners to the finish. Celestino had become the most expert of shots with Colt and rifle. He also had a flair for the knife, used at close quarters or thrown. He was as brave as the eagle he resembled.

Under the Rio Kid was Saber, who also had

'enlisted' in the cavalry when hardly more than a colt. The Rio Kid had picked him out, trained him, and he had become a marvelous war horse who would never stampede in the face of enemy fire, and was obedient to a word or touch of knee or hand.

Saber had a mirled eye which he would roll when angry. But with his friend, the Rio Kid, he was never cross. He was the fastest thing the Rio Kid had ever ridden, though his unprepossessing appearance fooled many.

Pryor and Mireles turned their horses up the lane to the ranchhouse which stood on a shaded knoll. A man was sitting in a rocking-chair on the veranda. The Rio Kid rose in his stirrups and sang out a greeting to him.

'Jo! Jo Walker!'

Jo Walker got up and came down the steps. He looked up into the Rio Kid's grinning face as they shook hands.

'Well, dang my hide if it ain't the Rio Kid! How are yuh, son?'

'We're in the pink, Jo, and we've stopped to see yuh. Heard yuh was livin' here with yore nephew. How's things?'

'Oh, fine, fine. Not so much excitement as used to be.' There was a tang of regret in Walker's voice.

*   *   *

He was past his prime but still stood six foot in

his bare feet. He was one of the greatest of mountain men, a comrade and peer of Kit Carson. His full name was Joseph Reddeford Walker but everyone called him 'Jo.'

Born in Virginia, Walker had reached the wild Frontier at an early age. He had been a trapper, a scout, and guide, with Benjamin Bonneville in 1832, exploring Great Salt Lake, the Humboldt River and the Sierras. He had lived with the Indians, and had guided Frémont's third expedition to California. He had run with the Fortyniners to hunt gold.

Brave in spirit, mild in manner, truthful and modest, Jo Walker was, as the Rio Kid put it, 'a man to ride the river with.'

Age had painted Walker's thick hair and clipped beard, and there were wrinkles in his nut-brown skin, but he had strength, plenty of it, in his powerful body. He insisted upon helping the Rio Kid and Mireles care for their horses, then led them into the pleasant ranchhouse. His nephew's wife brought cool cider and home-made cookies, and they began to talk together of the old times.

'What fetches you boys way down here?' inquired Jo.

'A mission,' replied the Rio Kid. 'Yuh savvy my pard here, Celestino, Jo. Well, he's got some cousins and an uncle in the Salinas country south of here. Or he did have.'

'Felipe Castro, brothair of my sainted mothair's.' Mireles nodded. 'But my uncle

21

Felipe ees dead.'

'He had a letter from one of Felipe's sons, his cousin Ygnacio,' explained the Rio Kid. 'Seems a sidewinder named von Wohl, with a gang of gunnies, cheated Castro of his ranch and killed him in the argyment. They wounded Pastor, Ygnacio's brother. The boys are with a relative named Guiterrez, in the Salinas Valley. But accordin' to Ygnacio this von Wohl hasn't let up. He's after Guiterrez now and there's been thunderation to pay.'

Jo Walker nodded.

'Been too much of that sorta thing,' he growled. 'Some fellers seem to think that the Californians in the south here can be cheated and killed, just 'cause they got Spanish blood in their veins. Sounds like von Wohl's that sort of reptile.'

'We're headin' for the Guiterrez rancho, Jo,' said the Rio Kid, 'and we aim to take a hand and see what von Wohl's got in the way of a scrap. Sounds interestin', don't it?'

'Shore does. I only wish—' Walker shrugged. His eyes flamed. 'If yuh need any help,' he finished, 'lemme know.'

The Rio Kid smiled.

'I figgered yuh might like the job, Jo. That's one reason I stopped. Yuh savvy this country back and forth.'

Jo Walker was still tough and strong.

'One last fling,' he murmured. 'I'll ride with yuh in the mornin', boys. Shore I savvy the

22

Salinas. I was all through there with Frémont and Kit.'

'From what young Castro wrote to Celestino,' went on Pryor, 'this von Wohl has ambitions. He's got a big gang together, and he's blazin' his trail through the valley, hittin' anybody he fancies. It may be a hard job to down him.'

'Now I wouldn't miss the fling for a million in gold dust!' cried Jo Walker. 'We'll chop this von Wohl down to size or lose our hair!'

In the morning they set out for the Guiterrez rancho with Celestino Mireles leading the way to his compatriot's home. He had asked directions to the rancho, asked in Spanish of a vaquero they had met soon after leaving Jo Walker's home.

'Ees not far now, General,' observed Celestino, as the Rio Kid and Jo Walker followed him on the winding dirt road which led them south through the fertile valley of the Salinas.

Below was the river. To the left rose low hills, and in uncultivated portions the wild mustard waved as high as fifteen feet in the summer breezes.

The Salinas was low at this season. At times it disappeared entirely in underground channels. Stretches of yellow sand gleamed in the hot sun.

The day was near its close as the travelers approached their destination. To the west, past the valley, the Santa Lucias now rose, cutting the Salinas country off from the Pacific.

'Mighty purty country,' commented Walker, from the saddle of the lanky black mustang he had ridden from his nephew's ranch. 'I been through here before, with old Kit and Frémont, but it's changed some from then. New folks comin' in and all.'

The Rio Kid looked over the lovely land. It held a soft magic and charmed him, nomad that he was.

'Worth fightin' for,' he said musingly.

* * *

The shadows were long as they turned into a private lane marked with the ranch brand of Don Joaquin Guiterrez. Lamps were lighted in the big hacienda that was well in from the road on the rise before them. The sun dipped behind the mountains, and dusk was at hand.

'' 'Alt! Stan' or I fire!'

The sudden challenge came, decided the Rio Kid, from the black clump of bush fringing the rail cattle fence which hemmed in the lane. The accent was soft. 'Answer him,' he said to Celestino.

'We are friends, senor, come to see Don Joaquin and the Castros, whose cousin I am,' Mireles sang out in Spanish.

'Your name?' demanded the hidden sentry.

'Celestino Mireles.'

'*Bueno.*' There was a boyish laugh. 'Come forward slowly. I am your cousin, Ygnacio Castro. Who are with you?'

Mireles switched back to English as he replied: 'The bes' of hombres, cousin Ygnacio. My *amigos*, the Rio Keed and Jo Walk-aire.'

They advanced, and soon Celestino was shaking hands with a slim, smiling young Californian, his cousin, Ygnacio Castro. There was sheer delight in Castro's welcome of his friend, and Ygnacio saluted Walker and the Rio Kid with the deepest politeness.

'Come, Celestino,' he said, 'we go to the rancho. I tak'you. We must keep guards out on all sides. Von Wohl, of whom I write you, ees a devil.'

'He's still botherin' you folks?' growled the Rio Kid.

'*Si, si.* Ees bad. But we talk of eet lataire. You mus' be tired, and hongry.'

Ygnacio had a horse nearby. Like most of his kind he never walked more than a few feet at a time. He led them to the entrance to the big hacienda. There was another sentry there, a tall young fellow whom Ygnacio introduced as Mariano Guiterrez, elder son of Don Joaquin. Mariano was older than Ygnacio and he was gravely handsome, with a dashing air and steady dark eyes.

He took charge of the guests, as Ygnacio returned to his post guarding the lane.

'You will honor me by coming this way,'

25

Guiterrez said, gesturing toward the home of the Don Joaquin family. 'It is not often we have such distinguished visitors.'

There was a winning smile on the man's lips and a twinkle in his eyes. The Rio Kid could not help liking him.

CHAPTER FOUR

BOND OF FRIENDSHIP

Mariano Guiterrez escorted the visitors through the wide gate into the patio, assisting them as they took care of the dusty horses. He then led the guests to a spacious hall which opened onto a great parlor in which were many people, men, women, children.

Among these was Pastor, Ygnacio's brother, his arm still in a kerchief sling. He greeted Celestino with deep affection. Jo Walker and the Rio Kid were introduced to the host and his friends.

Food, drink, the hospitality of the Californians, were showered upon them, and they were quickly made to feel at home. The Rio Kid tremendously liked these gracious, smiling folks, relatives and friends of his partner, Mireles.

Don Joaquin Guiterrez was an outstanding leader of them. His fine head was made for thinking, and his slender body, supple and graceful in his velvet clothing, was that of a born aristocrat. A ranchero of the old school, Guiterrez had a strong, determined character, a big-handed way with him.

There were other ranchers present, and the Rio Kid learned they were living there. Later

27

he learned that they were neighbors who had been dispossessed by von Wohl.

The loveliness of Teresa Guiterrez struck Bob Pryor. She was a jewel, in beauty and trimness. She wore a white silk gown, and a large comb in her dark locks. Donna Ysabel, Don Joaquin's wife, was a fit helpmate to the ranchero. She saw to the comfort of the guests, and helped to welcome them all.

For a time, seated in state in the great chamber, the Rio Kid wondered about the young fellow near him. His name was David Kenny—Don Joaquin had so introduced him. His blue eyes, watching Teresa a great deal of the time, were somber and somewhat wistful. He was sturdy, and seemed to be in the pink of physical condition. His light hair was thick, and he gave an impression of steadiness.

Chatting later on with Mariano Guiterrez, the Rio Kid learned that Kenny had clashed with von Wohl for the sake of the Castro boys. Since then he had remained with his new-found Californian friends and thrown in his lot with them. Kenny's intervention had saved Ygnacio and the wounded Pastor from death.

Although the menace of von Wohl hung over them, the southern Californians were happy, and their laughter reached the huge beams which supported the roof of the tastefully furnished hacienda. As soon as possible, the Rio Kid moved over to talk with Dave Kenny, whose looks he liked.

'Yuh've come to give us a hand, I hear,' said Kenny, his gaze steady and straight.

'That's right, Kenny. My trail-pardner, Celestino Mireles, had a letter from his cousin, Ygnacio Castro, tellin' of the trouble. We figgered we might help out. I savvy yuh're in sympathy with these people, since I heard how well yuh acted in the fight.'

Kenny shrugged.

'It was only what a decent man should do, Rio Kid. This von Wohl's poison. I'm glad you've come, and that you feel the way I do about our friends here. Von Wohl's been stirring up the tough elements with bad talk against them, saying they have no right here. But they're Americans just as we are, and fine ones too.'

The Rio Kid knew that Kenny had a sharp eye, and a keen, careful mind. He could tell that from the deliberate way Kenny had and the surety of his ideas. Kenny would be able to give him a clear picture of the situation in the Salinas land, an objective view. He asked the young fellow about it.

'Well, it's like this,' explained Kenny. 'Don Joaquin Guiterrez is or was wealthy, with plenty of cattle and horses. He owns a lot of land, but these folks have old Spanish grants. Some of them read, defining boundaries, "As far as the eye can reach" or "The circle a vaquero can ride in half a day," and so on. They don't hold up in court so well, not with thieving lawmen playing on prejudice and giving out lies.

'They're open-handed, too, and will give a friend in trouble everything they own. Why, Don Joaquin used to keep a big chestful of money under his bed. If a person who needed help come to him, he'd turn him loose in there and let him help himself!

'A couple of years back there was a bad drought, and the cattle died like flies. Rancheros had to borrow money to buy feed to keep their breeder stock alive. They signed anything, to get a little cash to keep on with. Von Wohl's got hold of some of them notes, buying them up, I understand. He's expert with a pen and has raised mortgages and notes, or even forged some.'

'How about the sheriff? Won't he help?'

Kenny frowned.

'The sheriff's an old fool, Rio Kid. I went to see him about the Castros. But von Wohl had got there first. You see, von Wohl had a dozen witnesses saying Castro had drawn on von Wohl, that the boys had opened fire on him when he come to collect a legal debt.

'The sheriff's is a political job, too, and von Wohl has power here. He's even a deputy sheriff! It's a fact. He's brought in a bunch of toughs from the mines, men who have been disappointed hunting gold and are desperate. He feeds them, gives them liquor and a dollar now and then, and they serve him. He's marshaled them like an army, too, with that accursed Hans giant of his.'

*　　　*　　　*

Von Wohl, Kenny went on, had settled at the Castro place, after dispossessing the owners. It was not far from the Guiterrez rancho, and the Prussian had henchmen posing as settlers who had squatted on what Guiterrez knew was his land.

'I'm worried,' confessed Kenny. 'Von Wohl, I believe, has a couple of Don Joaquin's notes. The polecats who run with von Wohl have been helping themselves to Guiterrez cows, running them off right and left—and cattle are the rancho's chief source of revenue. There's a lot of ground to cover. There've been some clashes, and a couple of drygulchings of Don Joaquin's vaqueros. It was my idea to keep out sentries at night.'

Kenny, the Rio Kid learned, was a Grand Army veteran. In fact, when Kenny found that the Rio Kid was the former Captain Robert Pryor, of Custer's staff, he realized he had heard of him.

'Fact is, I thought you looked familiar,' said Kenny. 'I'm sure I saw you once, when you were coming in from a mission behind the enemy lines.'

A strong bond was established between the two young men, and the Rio Kid knew he

31

could count to the end on Dave Kenny.

'This von Wohl needs some attention, no doubt of it,' said the Rio Kid, when he had drawn out all the facts at Kenny's disposal. 'I'd like to have a peek at the sidewinder, close to. Yuh say the Castro rancho ain't far from here. How about guidin' me over there this evenin'?'

Kenny looked at him quickly.

'You mean it? I could take you close, by back paths, but they keep guards out, too, and you'd never come through alive, Rio Kid. Von Wohl keeps a bunch of armed devils on hand and they're trigger-happy and full of red-eye most of the time.'

'Well, I got an idea. I want to jump in with both feet as soon as possible, and now's the best time to start anything. Von Wohl's enlistin' toughs from the mines. I'll fix up and act like one, get in and ask for a hookup with his bunch.'

Kenny thought that over in his deliberate way.

'You might get by with it,' he finally admitted. 'But if anything goes wrong they'll fill you full of lead, soldier.'

'Celestino, Jo Walker and you, if yuh're along, can cover me,' said the Rio Kid. 'I could give a whistle signal if it went wrong, and count on bluffin' or shootin' my way out.'

Pryor convinced Kenny, who had a brave heart. He motioned to Walker and Mireles, and the four slipped away, gathering in the

32

patio. Mariano Guiterrez was on duty at the gate.

'We're goin' for a little ride, Mariano,' said Kenny. 'We won't be long.'

'Mariano,' asked the Rio Kid, 'have yuh got one of them small picks or shovels like miners use? I might need it.'

'*Si, si.*'

Young Guiterrez went into a barn and brought out a short-handled miner's pick, and the Rio Kid hung it on his saddle.

'Careful,' warned Mariano, as they rode away. 'Von Wohl's keelers are out.'

'We'll watch.'

They paused to speak for a moment with Ygnacio, telling him to expect their return.

Kenny led them for a mile along the dirt road that wound south through the Salinas Valley. Now and again they could see the gleam of the moonlight on the river below. Then Kenny cut off the highway, up a slope to a trail which ran in the shadows of a long ridge.

They were strung out, and proceeded with trained scouts' precautions. After about an hour, Kenny pulled up, raising his arm to point at a lighted place below them.

'That's the old Castro rancho, Rio Kid. Von Wohl's taken it over.'

The soft night wind brought raucous sounds of drunken revelry at von Wohl's base of operations.

'I'm goin' down to the road and straight in, open-like,' said the Rio Kid. 'You boys come slower, and take to the brush. Creep in as close as yuh can, and be ready to rush in, in case I whistle.'

*   *   *

Signals arranged, the Rio Kid made quick preparations. He dirtied his face with earth, disarranged his gear, pulled a button off his shirt, and hung the miner's pick from his saddle-horn. Taking leave of his three friends, he worked down to the road and, mounting, boldly pushed toward von Wohl's headquarters.

He was not stopped while on the public highway. It was deserted, for the hour was late. It was after eleven o'clock when he reached the lane leading to the former Castro rancho, and swung the dun into it boldly. He hummed a snatch of a tune which was popular at the mines and on the road.

'Halt! Reach, cuss yuh!'

A shotgun *cluck-clucked* its warning from behind a stone pillar by the lane.

'Hey, there,' cried the Rio Kid gruffly. 'Don't shoot, pardner! I'm only lookin' for Mr. von Wohl's place. I'm from the mines—Smitty sent me.' He held up his hands, stopping Saber.

There was usually a 'Smitty' everywhere,

34

and he hoped the introduction might do to get him in.

'Strike a light and let's see yore face,' he was ordered, and he obeyed. 'All right,' the sentry said. 'Ride in slowlike, and sing out who yuh are when yuh come near the porch.'

CHAPTER FIVE

DANGEROUS VISIT

Bob Pryor rode slowly in. The sounds of wassail were loud in his ears. Men were drinking and carousing in the ranchhouse, and their horses stood outside. The Rio Kid could smell beef and coffee cooking, and also got whiffs of the raw brand of whisky sold in the mines and on the Frontier.

Near the long veranda fronting the adobe building, he cupped his mouth in his hands and called:

'Hi, in there! I'm from the mines! Is Mr. von Wohl home?'

Somebody on the porch, concealed in shadow, replied to him.

'Get down, feller, and come in. What's yore handle?'

'Roberts—Lew Roberts. I want a meal and a lodgin'. I was told I'd get it here.'

'That's right—providin' yuh're all right. Step in and ask for Hans.'

The Rio Kid dropped his reins. He took care that Saber stood to one side, out of the direct light. He had trained the dun himself, trained Saber to stand unless he whistled for him.

He went up on the veranda and through the

36

wide front door. The patio and the big living room were filled with men, roughs by the look of them, men in dirty trousers and shirts, and miners' muddy boots. Some wore felt hats or caps, others were bareheaded. All were drunk or on the way.

Mud and filth had been tracked in, and there was an evil smell about the place. The men all wore Colts and knives, and shotguns and rifles were stacked near at hand. Down one side of the main room a crude bar made of planks laid on logs had been set. About thirty men were up and doing, but the Rio Kid could see sleeping figures here and there, in the semi-darkness of side rooms.

Hard, red-rimmed eyes stared curiously at 'Lew Roberts,' and a huge man with a shaven, bullet head, small eyes and a hooked nose shuffled toward the Rio Kid. His hands, as large as hams, swung at his hips. A cartridge belt with two pistols and a knife was girded about his thick middle.

'You!' said the big fellow, in a thick accent that did not come from drink. 'Vot you vant, huh?' His puffy lips worked as he formed the words. That he was a German was obvious from his speech and appearance.

'My handle's Lew Roberts,' said the Rio Kid quickly. 'I'm from the mines near Sacramento. Sort of down on my luck and I got sick of diggin' for somebody else. They told me I could get lodgin', mebbe work, from Mr. von

Wohl.'

'Who told you?'

'Smitty. Pard I worked with there.'

'*Ja, ja*. Schmidt.' Hans rolled the name on his tongue, Germanizing it.

'Are you Hans?' asked the Rio Kid. 'They said to ask for Hans.'

'*Ja*, I'm Hans, Herr von Wohl's majordomo, *ja*. You got money?'

'A little. I can pay for likker and a bite.'

'*Gut*. Come on.'

Hans led him to the bar and they had a drink together.

There was meat and bread, and the Rio Kid, though stuffed after the meal at the Guiterrez rancho, managed to eat something. He was taking in the gathering, intending to remember the men he saw. Hans was plainly a tough customer, savage, but devoted to his master. 'Master,' the Rio Kid decided, was the only word for the relationship between Hans and von Wohl. And Hans knew how to handle such rough fellows as the Rio Kid feigned to be.

Hans showed no effects from the whisky he had been downing, and tried to draw the Rio Kid out in what he considered a clever manner. But Bob Pryor knew enough about mines and miners to answer Hans' supposedly tricky questions.

They had finished a second drink when the door at the end of the main room opened and

38

a man came in. Hans turned, blinking in the yellow lamplight.

'Here iss Herr von Wohl,' the big German. said. 'Vait. I talk to him for you.'

Hans lumbered over to von Wohl who stared glassily at the Rio Kid as his man spoke to him in a servile, fawning manner. Von Wohl nodded, and Hans beckoned the Rio Kid to approach.

Curious as to the fellow who had made such an evil stir in the Salinas country, the Rio Kid crossed over and stood before von Wohl, who inserted a monocle in one of his bulging eyes, which had the appearance of blue ice.

The face of the strong, square-bodied Prussian was cold, too. His wiry flaxen hair was clipped short and he had waxed the bristling mustache until the points stood straight in the air. A whitish scar slashed diagonally across his left cheek. He wore expensive clothes— whipcord trousers and a silken shirt, and his low boots gleamed with polish. A short-barreled revolver rode in an open holster attached to his wide belt.

*   *   *

He looked fixedly at the Rio Kid as Hans explained.

'He iss from der mines, *Herr* von Wohl,' Hans said. 'He iss name' Roberts. His friend iss Schmidt.'

'Yes, yes,' snapped von Wohl testily. 'You told me all that just now, Hans. Why must you repeat everything? Run along. I'll talk to this fellow.'

He did not relax his masterly air as he spoke with the supposed recruit. He held up his chin, and it was plain that there was insufferable egotism and vanity in von Wohl.

'How did you happen to come here?' he demanded.

'Smitty said I could find a job, mister.' The Rio Kid, eye to eye with von Wohl, sought to portray his role in a convincing manner. 'I'm sick of diggin' for other hombres.'

'You can handle a gun?' snapped von Wohl.

'Yes sir. I guarantee that. I can shoot and I can ride.'

'You may stay here tonight,' von Wohl said condescendingly. 'When I get to know you better, I'll consider taking you on. I have many men already but I could use a few more. Behave yourself, don't get too drunk, and ask Hans about anything you may wish to know.'

Von Wohl then abruptly turned away.

The Prussian troublemaker looked over the gathering. Then he went back through the door into the recesses of the hacienda. The Rio Kid, putting his small pack down in a vacant spot against the wall, rejoined Hans.

'Looks to be a smart hombre, that von Wohl,' he remarked.

'*Ja, ja.* He iss a great man, an officer!' Hans'

little eyes rolled. He sought to impress the recruit with his chief's importance. 'He hass fought in der armies of King Wilhelm of Prussia! A gendleman, he iss. In the old country you vould get off der sidewalk and bow vhen such a man passed. He hass plans, fine plans! He vill own diss Salinas land soon.'

'Mebbe he'll give me a job,' said the Rio Kid. 'Yuh reckon he will, Hans?'

'If you are all right. Soon ve know. Dere is work to do, for some fools oppose us and must be crushed.'

Hans had a keg of beer on tap. He kept a stein at hand and took long draughts from time to time, wiping his foamy lips with the back of his big paw. As they were talking, there was a slight stir at the front door, and from the corner of his eye the Rio Kid saw a man enter.

He was carrying a carbine in one hand, and wore crossed cartridge belts supporting twin pistols and ammunition. Over his shoulder was a strap to which was attached a pair of field glasses. He was a heavy fellow, with a dark beard, and he wore brown chaps, a dirt-stained sweat shirt, and a battered felt hat. He had just ridden in from some mission. He was weary, as he came to the bar.

The Rio Kid and Hans were looking at him, and he nodded to Hans.

'How goes der vatch, Gus?' Hans sang out.

'All right. Sort of tiresome, though, Hans.' The man's hard red-rimmed eyes had shifted

41

from Hans to the man standing at the far side of the German. He seemed to gulp, breaking his speech momentarily. 'Yeah, tiresome settin' out there all day. I need a drink.'

The Rio Kid was on the alert, and he had a keenly attuned attention. For just a breath, Gus had met his eyes full, and there had come a flash which Pryor thought was recognition, and fright with it. As Gus took a glass and bottle, pouring one for himself, the Rio Kid racked his brain.

'Now where have I seen this hombre?' he asked himself.

Gus was feigning to be at ease, as he chatted with Hans, and the Rio Kid could study the man. But for the life of him, though he had a keen memory for faces, Bob Pryor could not place this Gus.

'Diss iss Roberts,' said Hans, introducing the supposed recruit to Gus. 'He may join us, Gus.'

'Glad to meet yuh.' Gus nodded. He yawned then and downed the rest of his drink. 'Figger I'll get some shut-eye, Hans. I'm plumb tuckered out.'

He had the look and manner of speech of a miner and evidently he was a trusted aide of von Wohl's and a friend of the gang, but a warning was coming to the Rio Kid that the man was not a friend of his.

Over the Rio Kid's ribs was a scar from a battle wound which had healed unevenly.

For some reason or other, when danger threatened, it would itch, and now it was frantically calling for a scratch.

'Is the chief awake yet?' inquired Gus, as he started off. 'I better report.'

'*Ja*, he iss in dere,' replied Hans.

'See yuh later, mister,' Gus said, and nodded to the Rio Kid.

He strolled over to the closed door through which von Wohl had lately gone, opened it, and shut it after him as he went through it.

*   *   *

The Rio Kid hated to retreat. It was only a hunch that he had, from that flash in Gus's eyes and the instinctive hackles rising on his own flesh.

'I better check, though,' he thought, and said to Hans: 'What's that? Thought I heard a sentry call, Hans!'

The big German blinked. He was slow in comprehension at times.

'Huh? You heard someding? Vhere?'

'Over at the side, near that winder!'

Hans quickly turned from him and went to the opening to look out. The Rio Kid glided over to the door through which Gus had disappeared. He was in the cool and spacious dim-lit corridor before the puzzled Hans pulled his head inside the window.

An open door down the hall drew him with

its shaft of yellow lamplight. As he tiptoed toward this, he could hear the hum of voices. One speaker was Gus, the other von Wohl.

'I tell yuh, Chief,' Gus was saying, 'I seen this Roberts hombre ride up to the Guiterrez rancho just before dark this afternoon! He was with old Jo Walker, a feller I savvy, and a young Mexican. I don't know who Roberts really is but it looks mighty fishy. I was watchin' through the glasses, from the hill post.'

Von Wohl swore in German.

'He could be a spy, Gus. Just as I am about to deal Guiterrez the last blow, too! I wonder who he is? But I'll find out soon enough! I'll deal with him myself.'

A chair scraped. Von Wohl had hastily arisen. He was checking his gun.

'I'll shoot him if he raises a hair, Chief!' Gus said. 'Looks like he's come here to watch us. We better get him pronto.'

The Rio Kid hastily calculated his chances. At the far end of the hall, past von Wohl's office, was a heavy oak door with iron straps across it. It might be bolted from the other side. Besides, von Wohl and Gus were about to hurry from the office and they would see him if he rushed for the exit behind him.

'I'll have to go through von Wohl's winder,' he decided.

His swift mind worked with a cool precision, needing but a second-fraction to reach a decision. He was already moving toward the office, and his gun jumped to his trained hand with the speed of legerdemain.

'Hold it!' he snapped, the hammer spur back under his thumb as the Colt *cluck-clucked* its warning.

Von Wohl was almost in the lighted doorway. Just behind him was Gus, who had seen the Rio Kid approaching the Guiterrez hacienda. Gus was blocked from shooting by von Wohl's body. The Prussian rocked back on his heels, and the monocle slipped from the socket of his bulging eye.

'You—you pig-dog spy!' he gasped thickly.

The steady Colt hypnotized von Wohl. He drew in his breath sharply, held it for a long second. Sheer panic, yellow fear, flamed in his eyes and his face worked nervously.

'Don't—don't kill me!' he begged.

He held a short-barreled pistol in his right hand but it kept pointing at the floor.

'Drop it!' ordered the Rio Kid.

Now he was no longer the supposed recruit, a vagabond from the mines begging for work, but the Rio Kid, masterful, sure of himself. The flame in his eyes held von Wohl, told the Prussian, who had a keen brain, that he had come to grips with a powerful adversary.

The pistol thudded on the woven mat.

CHAPTER SIX

DIRECTIONS TO A HOT REGION

The room von Wohl used for an office was furnished with a flat-topped desk on which were inks and papers, chairs, a cabinet, and paintings were on the walls. Through an open connecting door a bedroom could be seen.

The office had two windows, and though the night was balmy, they were covered by heavy plush drapes. The windows in the bedroom likewise were curtained.

'You reach, too, Gus,' said the Rio Kid. 'I'll kill yuh both if yuh make a move, savvy? Hands up and back to that wall.'

He stepped in as they obeyed, and stood before the cowed pair in the light from the large lamp on the desk. Official-looking documents were spread on the blotter.

'Forgin' more notes and mortgages, eh, von Wohl?' said the Rio Kid. 'I hear that's one of yore specialties, along with killin' decent folks!'

Von Wohl gulped. There was a sickly tinge under his tan. He still expected to be shot down. Gus took it better. He was more taciturn and did not exhibit his fear.

'Who are you?' von Wohl asked the Rio Kid. He could not take his protuberant eyes

46

from Pryor's.

'I'll save yuh the trouble of snoopin' it out, von Wohl. Yuh'd soon find out anyways. My name's Bob Pryor, and they call me the Rio Kid.'

'Rio Kid.' Von Wohl repeated the name. 'I think I have heard of you, sir. What quarrel have you with me?' He began to pick up courage as he found that the Rio Kid did not intend to shoot unless forced to.

'My trail pardner happens to be a cousin of the Castros. You killed the old man and tried to finish off the sons. This is Castro property, which yuh stole. Now yuh're after Guiterrez. I'm here to serve yuh warnin'. I'm no gunny like them you hire but I can outshoot such. I'm givin' yuh warnin', von Wohl. Pull out of here while yuh're still alive and kickin'. If yuh bother Guiterrez or any more of these folks around these parts, I'll come after yuh, and I won't quit till yuh're done in!'

The Rio Kid's voice was not loud but it had a vibrant, steady quality which reached to von Wohl's soul. It was a clash of wills and, strong as was the Prussian's, he quailed before the Rio Kid.

'Maybe I'll take your advice, Rio Kid,' he said. 'Now what?'

'Now I'm pullin' out, through yore winder. Yuh'll see me again if yuh don't quit, von Wohl.'

The Rio Kid backed toward the heavy

47

curtains over the nearer office window. He meant to jump out, keeping the two men under his gun, and make his escape. Without taking his eyes from the men, who kept their hands up as long as his gun was upon them, Pryor swept the curtain aside with his left hand, stuck a leg up to thrust it over the low sill.

The two against the wall had an expectant air, and suddenly the Rio Kid realized why. His foot hit iron, the thick bars which had been cemented into holes drilled in the abode. The windows were barred!

It took him by surprise. The other windows, those he had seen, were not barred. Von Wohl, however, from fear of enemies, had taken this precaution.

Gus made a mistake then. The Rio Kid, startled by the trap he found himself in, took his eyes off Gus and von Wohl for a breath, and Gus threw himself to the floor, scrabbling for his Colt. He made it, sure fingers grasping the weapon. He whirled to fire at the Rio Kid but as he turned, Pryor let go and the heavy bullet knocked Gus flat on the mat.

Von Wohl was frozen in his tracks, stunned by the speed of his foe, the Rio Kid. He dared not move a muscle.

Gus was jerking spasmodically on the floor, dead, a .45 slug through the heart. His pistol had gone off but the lead had hit the wall several feet from the Rio Kid.

'How about it, von Wohl?' snapped Pryor, his eyes afire as he crouched, watching the Prussian. 'Want to try?'

Von Wohl gulped and grinned sheepishly. 'What—next?' he muttered.

Alive, von Wohl was valuable. Hans and the gang had heard those shots, and they were coming to von Wohl's assistance. The door down the way had banged open and men were rushing through the hall. The Rio Kid was trapped. There was only one chance to make it against so many guns.

'If yuh want to live, von Wohl,' ordered the Rio Kid, 'tell Hans to call them wolves back and keep 'em quiet till I leave. It's you first if I shoot.'

*　　　*　　　*

It would take an exceptionally brave man to resist in such a situation, to see his enemy die rather than save himself.

'Stay back, you fools!' von Wohl almost screamed as he called to his followers. 'Hans, pull them off. It is an order!'

'*Herr* von Wohl!' cried Hans, from the hallway. 'You are alife, *ja*?'

'I won't be if you don't obey me!' shouted von Wohl furiously. He kept his hands shoulder high, for the Rio Kid was back of him, Colt leveled.

Hans' great bulk showed in the hall, peering

49

curiously into the office. He saw von Wohl, his hands up, Gus lying still on the mat, the determined man with the pistol. Orders were orders with Hans, and he fully realized his master's peril. He turned and shoved back a couple of gunmen, swearing at them.

'Off mitt you! Back vhere you come from!'

He herded the ravening gang from the corridor to the main room.

'You start walkin' along the hall, slowlike, von Wohl,' ordered the Rio Kid. 'I won't kill yuh unless I'm set upon, savvy? I'm goin' to use yuh for a shield to get out of this den. Move!'

Von Wohl was tense. The ligaments stood out taut and white against the bronzed skin of his bull neck. His erect body was as stiff as a poker. Hands up, the Prussian walked down the hall as the Rio Kid directed.

Through the open door into the big room, fixed up as a saloon and sleeping place, von Wohl led the way. Hans had collected his men beside the bar across the way. They were all armed, and they had a silent but expectant air, like a pack of wolves sure of their kill.

The Rio Kid, back to the nearest wall, guessed they hoped to take him as soon as von Wohl was out of danger. He was close to the veranda exit now, inching along with von Wohl as a shield.

Sudden noises on the porch startled him. They must have hidden gunnies awaiting him,

50

to get him when he stepped from the light into the darkness. A muffled curse came from his left, and a Colt banged outside. Scuffling noises shook the boards of the long veranda and a shotgun roared.

'General! Thees way!' That was Celestino, close at hand.

There was a fight going on, a swift, violent clash. In the dimness, the Rio Kid was aware of struggling figures, of confused grunts, and powder flares.

Old Jo Walker was there, working hard and silently. Dave Kenny, too, with Celestino. They swept aside the von Wohl guards on the porch and rushed to the Rio Kid.

One of the plug-uglies with Hans went off half-cocked. He fired and a bullet tore splinters from the floor. Mireles, Jo Walker and the Rio Kid hit him a breath later, and he crumpled at Hans' spread feet.

'Stop it—stop it!' screamed von Wohl.

Hans was infuriated. He kicked viciously at the dead gunny who had disobeyed. Celestino and Walker jumped into the lighted room, guns up, covering the immobilized gang.

'They were layin' for yuh outside, Rio Kid!' cried Walker. 'We seen the polecats, and we come a-runnin'!'

'Dave,' the Rio Kid called to Kenny, who was on the porch guarding their backs. 'Fetch up the hosses!'

The angry eyes of the enemy burned with

51

rage. But Hans would not jeopardize his master's life. Walker watched, a dry grin spreading over his face.

'Look like a pack of disapp'inted kyotes,' he remarked.

The seconds ticked slowly away. There were enough von Wohl men there to overcome the few with the Rio Kid, but they dared not move. Those steady guns, and von Wohl in peril, held them. Hoofs clopped outside, and Kenny's voice reached them:

'Let's go, boys!'

Saber was near at hand. A whistle from the Rio Kid brought him to the steps. They took von Wohl out on the porch with them, and mounted.

'Stand where yuh are, von Wohl,' the Rio Kid said. 'I'll down yuh if yuh move before we're away. And remember—lay off Guiterrez or yuh'll hear from me again.'

'I'll remember, Rio Kid.' There was repressed shame mingled with the fury in von Wohl's voice.

The Rio Kid had made his soul shrink that night, and von Wohl's men had seen him cringe.

Jo Walker, Celestino, Kenny and the Rio Kid whirled their mustangs and galloped off. Von Wohl, as soon as he deemed it safe, threw himself down, rolling behind the low adobe balustrade. They could hear the Prussian shrieking:

'After them! Kill them!'

Wild bullets sought them in the darkness as they rode off.

*   *   *

Two days later, when the Rio Kid with the same companions, and with Mariano Guiterrez as well, rode into the sleepy little town of Soledad to gather more information, he learned something more about how far von Wohl's political ambitions had taken the man than Pryor had known before. The first thing that caught his eye as he rode into the settlement was an election streamer which ran from one side of the dusty street to the other.

The Rio Kid pulled up Saber, to read it. It was painted in black letters on a length of white canvas. Ropes were attached to cedar poles which had been sunk in the earth at either side of the road as it entered the confines of the town. And the streamer read:

FOR COMMISSIONER: COL. MANFRED VON WOHL THE PEOPLE'S CHOICE

'Von Wohl, he ees powerful,' observed Celestino. 'Weel not be easy to pull heem down, Rio Keed.'

'*Si*, he ees strong,' Mariano nodded, his handsome face grave.

The Spanish-Americans had felt the growing menace of von Wohl. Against his lawless tricks, however, they had been unable to organize an effective defense. They knew how evil he was, but those who had not yet been attacked by von Wohl were apathetic, concerned with their own troubles, as the general public is wont to be. The courts were ponderously slow. Von Wohl had clever lawyers, and he was gaining strength, backers.

'He's fooled some folks and scared others,' the Rio Kid said somberly. 'He'll win the election if he ain't stopped pronto. He's got plenty of punch.'

Alert, watching for von Wohl's gang, the riders moved on into the town of low lying adobe buildings and other structures. Californians in Mexican garb were enjoying the late afternoon warmth, and small brown children played in the street. Cantinas were filled. The stores were still open and a few belated housewives were buying provisions. Saddle horses, mules, and a few teams stood at the hitch-racks. There was a sheriff's office in the little brick jail at the corner of the plaza, which occupied the central part of the town.

But there was no sign of danger in Soledad, outside of the election posters. There were cards in some store windows or nailed to corral fences, advertising von Wohl's political aspirations.

Mariano Guiterrez had a black crayon with him. He amused himself by crossing out von Wohl's name on some of the posters. The Rio Kid, feeling coltish, borrowed the crayon and

54

wrote in large printed letters on a large sheet:
FOR THE NEXT TRAIN TO HELL:
VON WOHL.

The young men laughed, and Jo Walker, too, was amused.

'We'll carve that Prussian polecat down to size yet!' he vowed.

'Let's have a drink,' suggested the Rio Kid. 'I don't see any signs of the von Wohl gunnies—'

He stopped short at the sound of an angry voice.

'Say, what yuh doin', writin' on them posters!'

A tall figure, clothing flapping on his bony form, had turned the corner and was coming rapidly toward them. They waited, and the Rio Kid hastily sized up the man. The reddening light caught the five-pointed sheriff's star pinned to the sweated flannel shirt. Long legs were encased in stained black pants tucked into high boots. A battered felt hat rode back on his head, a few stray greasy locks showing, matted on his pale brow.

The lawman had a long, horselike face, with a thin, twitching nose and pale blue eyes. He needed a shave, and one dirty cheek was bulged out by his cud of tobacco. A walnut-stocked six-shooter rode at his bony hip.

'*Buenas noches*, Shereef!' cried Mariano. 'We do no harm. Only we feex eet as eet should be.'

'Well, behave yoreselves, or I'll run yuh in as public nuisances, Guiterrez,' growled the sheriff. 'Who're these fellers?'

'My *amigos*, Senores Walkaire, Mireles—you savvy Dave Kenny?—and Senor el Rio Keed. Ees Shereef Froleiks, *amigos mios*.'

Sheriff Froleiks craned his scrawny neck and peered at Bob Pryor.

'So yuh're the Rio Kid, huh? I've heard tell of yuh.'

'Good things, I hope.' Pryor smiled.

He had heard that Froleiks was stupid, a fool; and the man's appearance bore this out. The sheriff's eye was dull, his expression loutish, his voice was harsh. Either he was a tool or dupe of von Wohl's.

'That's as may be, mister. Just see yuh act like a gent in my bailiwick.'

'I always obey the laws of the land, Sheriff,' drawled the Rio Kid. 'That's more'n this von Wohl can say.'

CHAPTER SEVEN

ARREST

As the Rio Kid and his companions moved on, Froleiks stood looking after them. He was still watching them when they dismounted at *El Cantina Royale* and went in for a drink.

It was cool inside, with the wetted sawdust. A Mexican bartender, smiling at Mariano's quips, set up drinks. There were a couple of card games going on in the back, and the smell of tortillas and frijoles cooking mingled with the familiar damp odors of the saloon. Customers, in Mexican or Frontier garb, were at tables or along the bar.

Before turning his back, the Rio Kid checked the gathering. So did Mariano and Kenny, who knew many of von Wohl's followers.

'Looks all right,' said Kenny. 'I can't understand it, Rio Kid. Yuh shore threw a jolt into von Wohl. He ain't peeped since yuh called on him.'

That was true. For since that red-hot evening when the Rio Kid had gone to von Wohl's, the Prussian had not showed himself, and Hans and von Wohl's other men had stayed out of sight. There had been no further raids, no threats.

In that time, the Rio Kid had become better acquainted with Don Joaquin Guiterrez and the rest, with their problems and characters. They were the salt of the earth, open-hearted, decent. They wished only to be allowed to live in peace, to pursue their livelihood.

With Kenny, Jo Walker, and some of the younger men, the Rio Kid and Celestino had ridden far and wide across the beautiful Salinas land. Pryor had wished to get an idea of the long valley for which von Wohl was fighting, which the German sought to wrest from its rightful owners.

They had not clashed with von Wohl's faction. Nothing had been seen or heard of the Prussian's forces, and when the former Castro hacienda had been spied on from a distant hilltop no abnormal activity had been seen.

Soledad, too, was empty of enemies, so far as could be seen.

After they had quenched their thirst, Mariano Guiterrez spoke to Mireles.

'Come, Cousin Celestino. We go to the store and buy our supplies.' He had been told to pick up needed salt, coffee and other items.

Dusk was at hand now. The Mexican boy was lighting the lamps in the saloon. A warm breeze began to stir the dust of the plaza, as night fell.

'Reckon I'll go over to the store with yuh, and see if they got any new ribbons,' Dave Kenny said.

'For your hair, *amigo mio?*' inquired Mariano.

'No, for Teresa—' Kenny broke off, laughing at himself with the others.

The warmth, the peace of the ancient Salinas country soothed men's souls. It was difficult to feel that danger could be menacing here. It was a land of gracious living, of ease, and the Rio Kid felt its spell.

Kenny, Celestino and Mariano went off, jesting together. Jo Walker downed the last of his drink. 'I'm goin' to take that carbine of mine to the gunsmith, before he goes home to supper, Rio Kid,' he said. 'It needs a new hammer fitted.'

The Rio Kid was content to stay at the bar. He was relaxed, enjoying the soft strains of the guitar and the tenor voice of the Californian troubadour singing a love serenade when Sheriff Froleiks appeared. The Rio Kid watched him from the corner of his eye as the law officer came up beside him.

'S'pose we have a drink, Rio Kid?' said Froleiks.

'I'm not particular, Sheriff,' drawled Pryor.

Froleiks let that pass. He seemed eager to gain the Rio Kid's ear. Pryor watched carefully, for he did not trust Froleiks, but apparently the sheriff was alone. The Rio Kid did not see any of von Wohl's men on the porch, and the town had seemed to be clear.

'What's yore opinion of this mess between

von Wohl and Guiterrez?' asked Froleiks, as drinks were set up.

'I don't think, Sheriff; I know. Von Wohl's a rascal and outlaw and he'll bite the dirt. Guiterrez is a gent and an honest man. I'm with him, savvy?'

Froleiks cleared his throat, looking into the amber depths of his drink. At last he muttered, 'I got to think of votes, naturally.'

'Naturally yuh would.'

But Froleiks still seemed anxious, eager to stay on the right side of the Rio Kid who suddenly grew alert.

Another man had come in who glanced once at the Rio Kid, then walked on and to the bar and ordered. He was a sturdy fellow, around thirty. He had brownish hair which curled around his large ears, a blunt nose and wide-set blue eyes. He wore dark clothes, brown chaps, and a blue shirt. Twin six-shooters with black stocks were in his holsters. He was quiet and mannerly and paid no further attention to the Rio Kid, or anyone else for that matter, after a cursory glance.

'Has a lawman's look to him,' thought the Rio Kid, as Froleiks' unattractive voice droned along.

*　　*　　*

The stranger with the black-stocked guns had one drink, paid his score, wiped the lips of his

60

broad mouth with a blunt hand, and left the cantina without a backward look.

'Tell yuh what,' Froleiks was saying earnestly, 'I wish yuh'd come and talk this over, Rio Kid. Mebbe I been wrong all along. 'Course, when the judge orders me to serve papers, I got to serve 'em. That's understood, ain't it? 'Tain't my business to say what's right or wrong in such matters.'

'That's right, Sheriff. Still, yuh can draw the line helpin' snakes like von Wohl. What yuh wish to talk about?'

The Rio Kid was intrigued. Froleiks might, possibly, be trying to draw him into a trap. On the other hand, the officer might actually wish to be put on the right track. Guiterrez needed the law on his side. Von Wohl always saw to it that he himself had some legal standing in his outlawry, a forged note or mortgage, as well as witnesses to swear for him.

'I got some court papers just handed me today,' said Froleiks.

'Where yuh wan't to go?' asked Pryor.

"Well, the papers are over at my office. How about goin' there?'

'What've these papers got to say?'

'Yuh can see 'em. They have to do with the Guiterrez *rancho*. Von Wohl's goin' to take it over.' Froleiks had the air of being frank as he went on: 'If von Wohl knew I was tellin' yuh this, he'd never forgive me. He controls plenty votes, Rio Kid. Frankly, I want to win the next

61

election, for I reckon he'll be commissioner.'

'Provided he's alive and kickin' to comish,' the Rio Kid said dryly.

'That's it.' The sheriff nodded. 'Yuh can't blame a man for wishin' to be on the safe side, can yuh?'

So Froleiks was going to play along with both factions. There was some fearful respect in his washed-out eyes as he regarded the doughty Rio Kid. Probably he had heard of the fracas at von Wohl's.

'You lead the way, then,' suggested Bob Pryor.

His guns were in their holsters. He was not afraid of Froleiks, certainly, nor of any man for that matter. Close to the officer, a drygulcher would have a difficult time getting a bead on him, and there was no sign of von Wohl around Soledad.

Froleiks went out, and the Rio Kid, after a quick checkup with his eyes, trailed him closely across the plaza to the little adobe jail and office. Through the wide-open door a lighted lamp with a glass chimney which was standing on the oak desk showed that the office room was empty.

Froleiks went in first. He stooped, unlocking a drawer and taking out a sheaf of legal-looking documents.

A barred gate cut the cell-block off from the office. It was shut and no prisoners were in the block. The Rio Kid stepped into the office, went over and, careful to keep Froleiks in sight, glanced at the papers.

They concerned a legal seizure, calling for Don Joaquin Guiterrez to relinquish his properties to satisfy judgments held by Manfred von Wohl.

'All in order, yuh see,' said the sheriff.

'This is nasty, for Guiterrez!' growled the angry Rio Kid. 'I s'pose von Wohl furnishes the gunnies yuh use to drive out these folks yuh're cheatin'!'

And abruptly he recoiled, his brain reacting with the instinctive speed of a panther. He found himself staring into the barrel of a black-stocked six-shooter which was gripped in the steady blunt hand of a man who bobbed up from behind Froleiks' desk.

The Rio Kid might have taken his chance, fallen aside and made his lightning draw, but for one thing. In the first brief flash he had, he recognized the Federal marshal's badge pinned to the blue shirt. It was the sturdy fellow with the flat nose, the quiet man who had come into the saloon while Pryor had been talking with the sheriff. No doubt Froleiks had drawn him into conversation to point him out for the Federal officer.

Bob Pryor could not shoot a lawman. If the marshal was honest, he would not hold the Rio Kid. Pryor, the moment for his fight gone by, put up his hands.

'I'm Federal Marshal Ben Carmody, Tate,'

63

said the man with the gun. 'The jig's up. I been on yore trail all the way from Sacramento for the dirty killin' you and Gus Graves pulled there!'

*　　*　　*

Carmody was grave-eyed. His black-stocked revolver did not waver.

'Yuh're makin' a mistake, Marshal,' said the Rio Kid evenly. 'I'm Bob Pryor, known as the Rio Kid. I never heard of Gus Graves that I savvy and I did no killin' in Sacramento or elsewhere.'

'He's one of them smooth liars, Carmody,' snarled Froleiks.

'Read that,' ordered Carmody.

With his left hand he tossed a yellow paper, a telegram, on the desk so the Rio Kid could read it. It had been dispatched from Monterey to Carmody at Sacramento, and it said: BLACKJACK FRED TATE GUS GRAVES' PARTNER, BIDING HERE NEAR SOLEDAD AS THE RIO KID. WILL WATCH HIS MOVEMENTS WHILE WAITING YOUR ARRIVAL.

FROLEIKS, SHERIFF

' 'Twas a dirty job, shootin' that miner for his poke, Tate,' said Carmody. 'We had a description of Graves but not of the hombre who stood outside the winder and fired into the victim along with Gus. I found yore share

64

of the swag and the miner's watch in the saddle-bags of yore dun.'

'In *my* saddlebags?'

'That's it. Where you put 'em. The sheriff pointed out that mouse-colored cayuse of yores. He tried to bite my head off but we roped the cuss.'

The Rio Kid scowled at Froleiks. Now he knew that the sheriff was actually von Wohl's confederate. Froleiks must have planted the fatal evidence and arranged the trap, with the bona-fide Carmody to do the dangerous work of the arrest. Von Wohl prudently had remained out of sight, but his fear of the Rio Kid had prompted this trick.

'Get behind him and take his guns, Froleiks,' ordered Carmody. 'I'll keep him covered. Drill you if you move, Tate.'

With alacrity the lanky sheriff obeyed. He drew the fangs from the Rio Kid's holsters. Pryor had two more Colts under his shirt, and bided his time.

'Better let me talk, Carmody,' he said. 'I'm a law-abidin' man, which is why I didn't shoot it out with yuh. I can prove I'm the Rio Kid, not this Tate scoundrel.'

He recalled that the man he had downed in von Wohl's office had been addressed as 'Gus.' Perhaps Gus was the robber and killer. Von Wohl probably had taken the loot and planted it, through the connivance of Froleiks, in the Rio Kid's bag.

'Better watch out, Carmody!' cried Froleiks. 'He's got some tough pards in town with him and they'll shoot it out with yuh if they find yuh're holdin' him!'

'Yuh lyin' sidewinder!' said the Rio Kid. 'Yuh'll eat dirt for this, Froleiks.'

'Take it easy,' ordered Carmody. 'Hey—quit that!'

Froleiks was behind the Rio Kid. A blinding glare seethed through the Rio Kid's consciousness, and then blackness as he went down under the Colt barrel laid across his head by the sheriff.

CHAPTER EIGHT

PRISONER

Stars and a chunk of golden moon showed in the heavens as the Rio Kid returned to life. For it was night.

'Ugh—ugh!' he grunted, chiefly aware of his aching head, which felt thick, swollen.

He tried to raise his hand to touch his head, but found that his wrists were fastened together and tied with a thong to the saddle-horn in front of him. He was on a horse, jogging over a rocky trail. Black shapes of brush-clad mountains loomed to the right, but the land fell away on his left. He swallowed, his mouth dry as flannel, seeking to orient himself.

Ahead of him rode another man, a centaur shape on a dark, chunky horse. The man's felt hat and wide shoulders stood out against the sky. The creak of leather, the *clop-clop* of hoofs, the sliding of gravel and small stones mingled with the chirping of insects.

'Ugh!' The Rio Kid grunted again.

The man ahead turned. He had a lariat attached to one of the bridle rings of the horse on which the prisoner was riding.

'So yuh're comin' to! Want a drink?'

'Shore need one, Marshal,' the Rio Kid said

hoarsely.

It was Carmody, as sure of himself as ever. He pulled up, got down, and opened a metal canteen which he held to the Rio Kid's lips. The water felt good in Pryor's mouth and he drank all he could hold.

'Better save a little for breakfast,' advised the marshal. 'I ain't so shore when we'll fill up agin, Tate.'

'How—how'd we get here?'

Carmody chuckled. He drew out a tobacco sack and papers, he rolled two smokes, and thoughtfully stuck one in Pryor's mouth. He lit the Rio Kid's cigarette, then his own.

'Funny,' he said then, 'but that old goat of a sheriff seemed to think yuh belonged to him! I wouldn't trust him too far, not the way he behaved hisself. I had to take away his guns for fear he'd shoot yuh while yuh was knocked silly! I aim to deliver yuh back for a fair and square trial. 'Course it's a waste of time and money, for they'll hang yuh shore, Tate, but that's the law. Me, I believe in the law.'

Carmody had a bulldog tenacity, thought the Rio Kid. Once he got an idea, he held to it. He now was convinced his captive was a brutal killer. But the Rio Kid had a ray of hope. Carmody must be an honest officer, or he could easily have killed his helpless prisoner.

'Where are we now?' the Rio Kid asked.

'On our way back to Sacramento, Tate. I fooled that Froleiks cuss right and proper.

Bundled yuh on yore hoss and told Froleiks I was takin' the main road north. But soon as I made the first bend I cut off into the woods. We're on a hill trail, east of the highway. Reckon these are part of the Cabilans.'

The cigarettes glowed red in the night. Under the Rio Kid was Saber, his own horse, docile enough when in the presence of his friend, Bob Pryor. When they had finished the smoke, Carmody remounted and they jogged on.

'We'll take a snooze soon,' said the marshal chattily. 'I want to put some distance between me and Soledad. Froleiks was fit to be tied.'

An hour later Carmody stopped again, and this time they camped. The marshal handcuffed the Rio Kid to a sapling, and permitted him to sit down, back to the little tree, and try to doze. He staked Saber, and picketed his own mustang, a powerful black gelding with a star on his forehead.

Carmody was wary. He had no intention of letting his captive escape. He sat down facing the Rio Kid, and feigned to go to sleep but every so often would open his eyes for a peek.

The first gray of dawn found the Federal officer up. He had another canteen of water, some hardtack and jerked beef, and he shared these with the prisoner, chatting in a friendly enough manner but always alert.

The Rio Kid felt stronger. The ache in his head was subsiding although the head was still swollen and he had lost his hat back in Soledad.

'Sorry about yore Stetson,' said Carmody. 'It fell off at Froleiks' and I forgot it in the rush. I'll pick yuh up another soon as I can.'

He arranged the Rio Kid for riding again, rope tied to Saber's ring, hands fastened to the horn. As the new day came up, the Rio Kid looked in vain for landmarks, but the country was unfamiliar. Jo Walker and Celestino and he had ridden south from Monterey on the main Salinas route, whereas Carmody was following a parallel but less frequented trail.

*   *   *

As the sun peeped over the Cabilan range, on their right, they emerged from the hills onto a great plateau stretch covered with short, brown grasses which curled low to the dry ground. As far as they could see this tableland spread north and westward. There were no trees, no large rock formations to break it, and the morning wind blew at will across the expanse. Mists over the Pacific, many miles west, were beginning to dispel. Somewhere in that area lay the Salinas and its main valley.

'Huh,' growled Carmody, disappointedly, as his eye roved ahead. 'Don't seem to be anything like water for miles around. I was hopin' we might find a spring. Oh, well, we'll have to make the dregs in the canteens do. I ain't goin' back for nothin'.'

It was a dry march. The Rio Kid, with Carmody's help, tied his bandanna over his head against the sun, but as it rose to noon position, his head became hot and began to ache furiously, his eyes smarting from strain.

'This country looks plum useless,' complained Carmody. 'Doggone, Tate, I got to have water. We'll cut west, and try to reach the river valley. I reckon we're far enough away from Froleiks' bailiwick now.'

It was nearly two hours before the suffering horses, with their equally dry riders, came to a small rill which issued from a rocky bluff at which the vast plateau ended. They had to dismount and help the animals down a long, steep slide, in order to reach the water.

*　　　*　　　*

For a time they rested, then Carmody said:

'We'll hit the main road now. Come on.'

The late afternoon was upon them when they came out on the route highway leading to Monterey and points north. They had not made many miles from Soledad, for their wanderings had taken them far out of line.

Rounding a bend in the road, with a clay cut overgrown with brush on their right, Carmody suddenly jerked his black to a stop. Looking past his captor, the Rio Kid saw riders coming toward them at a sharp clip. There were a

71

dozen in the van, perhaps more behind in the clouds.

'*Adios*, Carmody,' drawled the Rio Kid, with grim humor. 'Here's von Wohl and his bunch of merrymen, huntin' us. They'll down you along with me.'

His hands secured, he could only await death.

'Shucks,' growled Carmody. 'Where's this von Wohl fit in?'

'It's his show, Marshal. Yuh've been used for a job von Wohl was afraid to try hisself, namely, to down yores truly. There he is, von Wohl, in the center. The one with the square head. That big hombre is Hans, his chief helper. There's Froleiks, too, on the left.'

They had been seen. Men in the lead set up a cry, pointing at the dusty pair stopped in the road. Carmody cursed. Hastily he snatched up a double-barreled shotgun from a socket in which it rode, and cocked both triggers.

'They ain't takin' yuh away from me,' he growled.

'Yuh'll have trouble holdin' that howlin' mob, Carmody. Better let me help.'

Carmody was shaken. 'If I let yuh loose and give yuh a gun, will yuh promise to go on back with me—provided we *can* ride?'

'All right—if that's the way yuh feel.'

'I do. I'd as soon die as lose a prisoner.'

Carmody was hastily releasing the Rio Kid. He had taken away the guns hidden under

Pryor's shirt, having searched him while he lay unconscious. But he had the Rio Kid's cartridge belts with the holstered Colts, and he tossed them to Pryor, who quickly buckled them on. The Rio Kid worked his fingers, getting the kinks out, for the ropes had cut off circulation and his hands ached.

Froleiks, Hans and von Wohl were surrounded by their henchmen.

'Hi, you!' shouted the sheriff. 'We want that there prisoner, Carmody. Been chasin' yuh all day.'

They had taken the main road in the darkness, and kept going, but seeing no sign of the Rio Kid and his captor, they had doubled back, only to run into the pair. The menacing eyes of Carmody's shotgun, loaded with buck, stared at them and they prudently pulled up at twenty-five yards, sitting their saddles.

'This hombre is *my* prisoner!' sang out Marshal Carmody. 'I'll defend him. I've give him his guns so's he can help. Stand out of my way.'

'See here, Marshal,' called von Wohl. 'We have a warrant for Tate's arrest on a killing charge. You must turn him over to us.' He waved a white document.

'I'm a Federal officer,' replied Carmody, 'and Federal law comes first. If yuh got any charges, make 'em at Sacramento, where I'm takin' him.'

'That's foolish,' argued von Wohl. 'If it's

73

worth anything to you, Marshal, I'll pay you double the reward on his head, here and now. Save you a lot of trouble.'

*   *   *

The Rio Kid smiled to himself. Carmody was not the type to be bribed. He watched the brick-red hue come up under the marshal's bronzed hide.

'Why, yuh dirty cuss!' frothed Carmody. 'I ought to pepper yuh with buck for that. You can't buy me!' He had a stubborn streak, and his own idea of honor. 'Out of my way. Yuh're holdin' up a Federal officer, von Wohl.'

Stragglers from von Wohl's posse kept riding up to join the main party. Von Wohl consulted with Froleiks and Hans.

'Very well, Marshal, you win,' he said to Carmody. He waved his riders off to one side, so that Carmody could pass on the road.

'That won't do, von Wohl,' said Carmody, who was no fool when it came to strategy. 'Take yore men off across that field, see, to them woods.'

The woods were far enough away from the road to make accurate shooting difficult, so if the gang tried for them they would have a fighting chance.

'Their hosses are jaded, Carmody,' murmured the Rio Kid. 'If we get a head start we'll be all right.'

74

'That's what I'm playin' for,' the marshal answered as he nodded.

But von Wohl and his men, too, realized they could not overtake the swift mustangs of the Rio Kid and Carmody. A line of riders, ordered out by von Wohl and led by Hans, swung off as though to go to the woods, but instead dug in their spurs and raced parallel to the highway, seeking to ring Carmody and Pryor.

It was vital to act quickly. The Rio Kid and Carmody whirled their mounts, at the same time hastily firing. Already von Wohl's faction had begun shooting, seeking to overrun them and down them by sheer weight of numbers.

The blasts of Carmody's shotguns, hurling spreading buck, the snapping Colts of the Rio Kid, cut into the galloping gunnies. One flew off his horse, another shrieked and slumped in his leather. A mustang crashed, throwing a third man off into the grass.

The leaders veered out, their bullets kicking up dust and shale. Von Wohl and Hans, shooting from up the road, were bellowing orders above the din.

But von Wohl and Hans made no attempt to charge the Rio Kid and Carmody. The Prussian had swung out of the saddle to get to safety behind his mount. Twenty-five yards still remained between him and the Rio Kid, who certainly did not want to kill a bronc in order to shoot a man down.

Besides, there was much else to attract the Rio Kid's attention. His guns blasted again and again at the gunmen who tried to get past him, and they were failing.

CHAPTER NINE

TWO AGAINST MANY

Having turned the charging line, the Rio Kid and Carmody ducked back around the bend. Carmody led the way up a steep trail away from the road which straightened out here, with no cover in sight for a mile. It was good tactics, for von Wohl would have the advantage in the clear.

'We'll take cover!' called Carmody. 'Up above, Tate.'

There were rocks and brush to serve them, and at the top of the steep rise they dismounted, leading their horses into a safe spot. Turning, they could rake the road with their fire, and von Wohl's men soon found it out. Over-eager gunnies felt the sting of lead and retreated, howling in baffled fury.

At von Wohl's direction they circled around, and the two crouched in the rocks could see them, out of easy pistol range, starting up in order to work behind the pair.

'Better move, Carmody,' said the Rio Kid.

'Let's go,' Carmody agreed. 'See that patch of trees behind us, Tate? We'll make it next.'

They beat the enemy to it, and again made a short stand, holding off the stubborn foe. The afternoon was fading, as they fought and ran, von Wohl always shoving them back into the wilds, back toward the east.

It was not until dark fell that they succeeded in eluding their pursuers. Then they could mount, in the silver moonlight, and they rode as best they could cross country. Carmody was worn out, panting. His eyes would scarcely stay open.

'I'm plumb done in, feller,' he growled. 'I got to sleep.'

'Me, too,' said the Rio Kid.

They could no longer hear the calls of their opponents, as von Wohl's men sang out to one another. They hid in a black patch of woods, and the Rio Kid took off his gunbelts.

'Here yuh are, Carmody, if yuh want 'em. I give yuh my word yuh'd get 'em back.'

Carmody waved the guns aside.

'Never mind now. Let's sleep . . .'

Up at the first hint of dawn, the Rio Kid and Carmody ate iron rations, then drove on north. They were near the rim of that great waterless flatland which stretched east and south as the sun came up. A haze hung over the vast plateau.

Hour after hour they rode and finally, two days later, Carmody rode his limping horse into the old Spanish town of Monterey with the Rio Kid at his side. They had been slowed by difficult going in the wilderness, by ravines, rocks and woods, for Carmody had insisted on sticking to the bush, after the fight with von

Wohl.

The Rio Kid loved and admired the old settlement, standing on the bay of the same name. Spanish settlers had built it long years ago in an amphitheater made by the gently sloping hills, clad in dark pines. The Franciscans had erected a mission there.

Before the coming of the Yankees, Frémont, Kit Carson, Jo Walker and the rest, Monterey had been the gayest, most ambitious of all California towns. With the adobe brick homes, the plaza and the buildings of the ancient presidio, Monterey had a quaint aspect, and a drowsy contentment with life hung over it.

It was cool in the early morn as the two bedraggled horsemen moved slowly along the dusty main way. Carmody was an iron man, but he was done in. With his wiry soldier's physique, the Rio Kid had stood the ordeal better than the marshal.

'Hot food—that's what I want first, then a real sleep,' muttered Carmody.

He blinked with his red-rimmed, haggard eyes at the man who had come with him. He shook his head. 'I don't savvy it,' he said.

The Rio Kid knew what he meant. Carmody couldn't savvy how such a good trailmate and fellow as his captive had turned out to be could commit a cold-blooded killing.

Pryor had given up arguing with the marshal, for Carmody was still sure that he had the right man. But now the Rio Kid said, with a faint smile:

'There's a telegraph office here, Carmody. How about wirin' to Sacramento? Mebbe there's some news that'll convince yuh I'm the Rio Kid and not Tate.'

'I hope what yuh say's right,' said the Federal marshal. 'I wish yuh wasn't Tate. I'd hate to see yuh strung up, feller.'

Carmody thought enough of him to go to the telegraph office and send the wire. Then they left their horses at a livery stable and walked to a restaurant just opening its doors for the morning meal. Ham and eggs, hot coffee, rolls disappeared from before the two stalwart young men. Finally Carmody gave up.

'Woof! That was swell, Tate. A smoke, and then we'll sleep.' He loosened his belt, and began rolling a cigarette.

*　　*　　*

A party of men came into the place, and sat down at a nearby table. The Rio Kid turned to look at them.

'Yuh savvy who that is, Carmody?' he said then. 'He's Leland Stanford, the feller who built the Central Pacific railroad and joined up with the U.P. He's a friend of mine. He'll tell yuh who I am.'

'Yeah?' Carmody mused, opening his sleep-drenched eyes. 'Shore enough. That is

Stanford. I've seen him around.'

Stanford was a tall man with a portly body. He weighed over two hundred and fifty pounds. A clipped beard covered his strong jaw, he had keen eyes, and was an elegant dresser. There were touches of gray in the former governor's thick hair. Stanford had held California for the Union during the Civil War. But right now Stanford was interested in railroad building.

He was deep in talk with another big man, even taller than himself, though not quite so heavy. Shrewd, deep-set eyes were riveted to Stanford's. This companion of the former governor wore well-cut modern clothing.

There were three other men in the party, the two who were wearing whipcord pants and outdoors shirts having the aspect of engineers. At a question from Leland Stanford, one of them took a folded sheet from his pocket and spread it out on the table, so that Stanford and his friend could consult it.

'Let's go speak to Stanford,' said Bob Pryor.

Carmody, spurs clinking, trailed him over.

'Good mornin', Guv'nor Stanford!' said the Rio Kid.

Stanford was poring over the sheet. It was a large-scale map. He looked over his shoulder with a frown, but it turned quickly to a smile.

'Well—it's the Rio Kid! How are you, sir? What are you doing in Monterey? Sit down and have some breakfast with me.'

81

The Rio Kid pulled up a chair, and Carmody stared, jaw dropped as Stanford began introducing Pryor to his friends.

'This is my partner, Collis Huntington.' He was the big fellow with the deep-set eyes. 'Mark Hopkins, General Rawson, our chief engineer, and Major Ord, assistant chief engineer.'

Stanford signaled the waiter, ordered food and drink.

'This here is Marshal Ben Carmody of Sacramento, Guv'nor,' the Rio Kid said. 'He has an idea in his head that my real name is Tate. Fact is, he's got me under arrest.'

Carmody was uncomfortable under Stanford's cool scrutiny.

'Well, the evidence—' he said lamely.

'Nonsense! You've made a mistake, Marshal. However, 'tis human to err.' Stanford enjoyed giving out such platitudes, and did so with an air of having originated them.

Huntington had little to say. Born in Connecticut, he had worked his way up from poverty to a great fortune. He had tried gold mining when he had come West but had quickly given it up and opened a store in Sacramento. From this he had entered railroad building with Stanford and his own business partner, Mark Hopkins.

'I been in the Salinas Valley,' explained the Rio Kid. 'Bumped into a scoundrel there named von Wohl, who's busy cheatin' and killin' folks so's he can seize their land. I was just startin' after him good when Carmody came along and arrested me.'

'How about the sheriff?' asked Stanford. 'Can't check this fellow?'

'The sheriff's in cahoots with von Wohl, who makes shore he's in the clear, Guv'nor, with legal papers. He's a first class forger, this hombre is.'

'Sounds bad.' Stanford thought for a moment. He had been covering the map with his arms, but he raised them and turned the map toward the Rio Kid. 'You see this? It's a map of the Salinas country.'

'Stanford!' snapped Huntington. 'Don't you think you're being indiscreet?'

'No. Our surveyors are already at work, Huntington.' To Pryor Stanford said, tracing a line penciled on the map: 'This is the intended route of the railroad we are about to push through the Salinas Valley.'

A light burst upon the Rio Kid.

'Well, I'll be hanged! Now I savvy what von Wohl's up to. Yuh're buildin' a station at Soledad, and yore line runs through the west section of the Guiterrez ranch! Castro's, too! A railroad ups the price of land and von Wohl cleans up a fortune!'

'No doubt this fellow heard of the projected line.' Stanford nodded. 'There've been leaks, likely, and with the grants being made and our surveyors actually at work, everybody will soon know it.'

*   *   *

Carmody was still standing there, shifting his weight from one foot to the other.

'I'm goin', Rio Kid, but I'll be back pronto,' he growled, and stalked out.

Carmody was waiting for the Rio Kid an hour later, when Bob Pryor emerged from the restaurant with Leland Stanford and his party. An elegant equipage, drawn by two pairs of sleek black horses, awaited Stanford and his friends.

'I'll see what I can do to help out, Rio Kid,' promised Stanford. 'There must be a way to check von Wohl.'

'Thanks, Guv'nor.' The Rio Kid shook Stanford's hand and nodded to Huntington and Hopkins, and the two engineers who were already climbing into the vehicle.

The Rio Kid could not count too heavily on such busy personages. Stanford was immersed in his work, rushed day and night with details and great matters. Von Wohl, too, operated behind a screen of legality, with court orders and the sheriff. By the time an investigation could be made, it would be too late to save Guiterrez. Von Wohl had plenty of power in the Salinas country.

When the railroad men had driven off, Ben Carmody shuffled over to the Rio Kid and stared shamefacedly at the erstwhile captive.

'I got an answer to the wire I sent,' he said. 'They captured Blackjack Fred Tate the other day. There was a gunfight and Tate was mortally wounded. He confessed that killin', done with Gus Graves. Graves had the watch and some of the loot with him. I been a dumfool and I owe yuh an apolergy.'

'That's all right, Carmody. Lucky we got through the way we did. Soon as I'm rested, I'll head back to the Salinas.'

'If yuh can use another gun, I'll go with yuh,' offered the marshal.

CHAPTER TEN

LOST RANCHO

It was a grim moment when Dave Kenny stared from the gate at the array of armed men Manfred von Wohl and Sheriff Froleiks had brought to the Guiterrez ranch.

'Zey hav' seexty, or more,' Don Joaquin, at Kenny's side, said. 'Hold fire vaqueros, and I weel ask what zey weesh.'

Mariano Guiterrez was near his father, and the Castro boys were with other armed vaqueros. They would fight for the ranch against von Wohl.

The morning was bright and lovely, sweet with the perfume of flowers and shrubs. The Salinas Valley seemed at peace—but von Wohl had come.

Kenny had an uneasy feeling. He needed sleep, for he had helped the frantic Celestino Mireles and Jo Walker in the fruitless hunt for the Rio Kid who had so mysteriously disappeared off the face of the earth. For days they had searched the environs of Soledad and the range, for some sign of their friend, but without success.

Mireles would not sleep, save in snatches. Even now he and Walker were out somewhere, still looking for the Rio Kid. They had visited von Wohl's, peering in at the former Castro hacienda, but they had been fired on by the guards, and had seen nothing to indicate that von Wohl had the Rio Kid a prisoner. In fact, during the first couple of days, they had observed that von Wohl's patrols evidently were on a manhunt themselves.

At last Kenny, Mariano and the rest had concluded that the Rio Kid was dead, and had been tossed into some brush-choked gully for the buzzards to pick. But Celestino and Jo Walker refused to accept the theory. And now had come more tragedy.

'Eef you come closer, we weel shoot!' Don Joaquin shouted to the invaders.

Von Wohl, Hans, and the hard-faced riders with them had stopped their advance. Sheriff Froleiks raised a white cloth and waved it back and forth, at the same time riding his horse from one side to the other, indicating he wished to parley.

'Be careful of a trick,' warned Kenny.

'*Si*. I see what he want, however.'

Don Joaquin waved back and Froleiks, his stained face working nervously, gingerly approached. He held some white documents in one hand and waved his flag of truce as he came to meet Don Joaquin.

'Look here, Guiterrez,' said the sheriff, 'I got legal papers to serve on yuh. This gunplay yuh been puttin' up is agin the law. Yuh got no right to threaten an officer. Them fellers is my posse, savvy, duly sworn in to enforce the law.'

'Law!' fumed Don Joaquin. 'You mus' know von Wohl ees keeler and thief!'

Froleiks thrust the papers into the Spanish-American's hand.

'Read 'em. Yuh failed to appear in court and von Wohl's got a seizure of yore land by default. They're all legal-like, them papers. Yuh got to move, Guiterrez.'

'You're crazy!' growled Kenny, who had overheard the talk. 'You can't take a citizen's property from him without even a hearing!'

'Keep yore oar outa this, Kenny, or I'll run yuh in,' snapped Froleiks. 'Yuh're playin' with fire, my boy. Better pull out while yuh got the chance.'

Don Joaquin was reading the documents. There was a bewildered frown on his face.

'Yuh got no time to fool away, Guiterrez,' said the sheriff. 'Pack up and get.'

Froleiks waved the cigar he was smoking.

Kenny was furious. He knew there had been cases where rancheros had been tricked out of their properties, that they were prodigal with their money and careless about notes and mortgages. But von Wohl's method was the rawest he had ever heard of.

He stood by Don Joaquin as the ranchero shuffled through the copies of legal papers. One was a deposition signed by Sheriff Froleiks to the effect that he had served papers ordering Guiterrez to appear in court on a date some three weeks before.

'They've forged and lied,' growled Kenny. 'Don't give in, Don Joaquin. Let's fight.'

'I weel not surrender!' declared Guiterrez.

Froleiks was turning to leave. One of his saddle-bags slipped its buckles and fell to the dry grass.

'Say, Froleiks, you dropped something!' called Kenny.

Mariano Guiterrez gave a sharp cry. He raced out past his father and Kenny. Now Kenny saw the thin gray streamer of smoke hissing from the closed flap of the bag which the sheriff had let fall. He started forward to help Mariano, but the young man seized the saddle-bag and flung it away.

It landed in the area between the hacienda and von Wohl's forces. Some of the Prussian's men hastily jerked their reins to retreat, but von Wohl threw up a heavy-caliber rifle and fired.

*   *   *

Mariano had just straightened up, to shake a triumphant fist at the attackers, when von Wohl's bullet hit him. It knocked him over on his back, and blood spurted from his chest.

Don Joaquin uttered a shrill cry of anguish. Women screamed from the barred hacienda windows. Mother and sister had seen Mariano fall. Kenny and Guiterrez started forward, and

89

at that moment the saddle-bag exploded with an ear-shattering roar. It was a small bomb which Froleiks had dropped there, concealed in the bag. He had touched off the fuse with the cigar he had been smoking.

Dust billowed into the air, and there was a pattering of falling pebbles and dirt as Kenny and Don Joaquin, sent to their knees by the shocking blast, fought to clear their brains.

Kenny, young and strong, was first to recover. He got up, staggered to the spot where Mariano lay, gasping for breath, blood staining his silken shirt front. The dust screened Kenny as he picked up the brother of the girl he loved and started back into the house.

'I've got him! Don Joaquin! Look out, they're charging!'

Von Wohl was ordering his men to take the hacienda. Hoofs shook the earth as Kenny, with Mariano slung over his shoulder, urged Don Joaquin inside. They slammed the gate.

'Fire!' Guiterrez cried.

A volley roared, and von Wohl's gunnies swerved, feeling the sting of the defenders' lead. They shot as they flew past, but circled and drew up at a safer distance.

As soon as it was plain the charge had broken, Kenny hurried into the cool interior of the hacienda, where they had carried Mariano. Teresa, tears streaming down her soft cheeks, and Donna Ysabel, kneeling at the side of her stricken son, were in the bedroom.

Mariano was unconscious. His breathing rasped, and his mother was trying to staunch the flow of blood. Don Joaquin was tense, his face a gray mask.

Again von Wohl threw his circle about the hacienda. Those inside it were under siege. For two hours, Donna Ysabel and her husband, aided by all those in the ranchhouse, tried to stop Mariano's bleeding. It was down to a trickle now, but he was sorely wounded.

'He must have a doctor, and quickly,' declared Donna Ysabel.

The parents were frantic. So was Teresa, whom Kenny sought to comfort.

'Von Wohl won't let anybody through,' Kenny said soberly. 'He knows Mariano's badly hurt, if not dead.' But Kenny knew there was no mercy in the Prussian.

He heard a loud, magnified voice echoing from the hacienda walls. Von Wohl was shouting at them through an improvised megaphone.

'Listen to me, Guiterrez! You have just half an hour to decide whether you live or die. You are breaking the law by refusing to surrender this property to me, its legal owner. We have explosives and we will start hurling them into your house if you do not leave.'

With slings, they could catapult bombs into the courtyard, over the walls, or onto the flat adobe roof. Women, children, and the fighters inside would die or be maimed. The heart had gone out of Don Joaquin when Mariano had fallen, and the fact that von Wohl's gunnies prevented their reaching a doctor or surgeon who might save his son's life crazed the ranchero.

'We must give up, so we may save Mariano!' cried Donna Ysabel.

Don Joaquin nodded.

'*Si*. I care for nozzing, eef we cannot save heem.'

Kenny could not blame the parents. Many innocents would be injured and killed if von Wohl carried out his threat of throwing the explosives. The young Pennsylvanian trailed Don Joaquin to the barred gate, where Guiterrez called out to the enemy.

Froleiks approached, with several tough gunnies.

'Yuh willin' to quit, Guiterrez?' the sheriff asked.

'We weel go, eef you draw off and do not attack us,' replied Don Joaquin.

Froleiks went back to confer with von Wohl. The Prussian evidently was satisfied. He answered through his megaphone, his heavy, crass voice dinning in their ears with its ring of victory:

'Very well, Guiterrez! Get your people out fast, though. You have twenty minutes. If you attempt to trick me, we'll cut down everyone of you.'

Kenny dug his nails into the palms of his hand. There was contempt in von Wohl's voice, contempt for the people he was robbing, the pioneers who had settled California. The Prussian looked upon them as his inferiors, to be cheated and cast out.

To save Mariano, to protect the women and children, Don Joaquin was relinquishing his great rancho. And once von Wohl was in possession, he would be hard to dislodge.

*   *   *

Kenny watched, to make sure that von Wohl actually pulled off his ravening crew. The Prussian led them away, to the southern hill a half-mile off. Here it was that Kenny and the Castros had fought von Wohl, and Guiterrez had brought his vaqueros out to save them. The gunnies dismounted. They had liquor, food and smokes, and they waited as the exodus from the hacienda began.

Don Joaquin and others carefully placed Mariano in a spring wagon, and started off for the home of a doctor, a former Army surgeon in the war, who lived on a ranch a few miles northeast of town. Donna Ysabel went along, to care for her son.

Kenny and the rest hastily packed what they could in wagons or bags as they prepared to leave the hacienda. Some of the young vaqueros, armed with carbines, pistols, and lassos kept a sharp eye on von Wohl, but there was no interference. Von Wohl, who knew that hired fighters such as he bossed could not be counted on when resistance was too hot, was content to let the people leave the rancho.

With women and the children in the shaded wagons, along with bags of provisions and a few personal belongings such as clothes and jewels, they streamed out the gate. The vaqueros formed a rear guard to protect the train. Kenny hung back with them.

Teresa was with her aunt in one of the buggies. The girl, like all the rest, was intent on saving life. The property must be left to the mercy of von Wohl.

They started away on the road, and turned north. Kenny and the vaqueros, with guns ready, watched as von Wohl took possession of the rancho, riding in as soon as the owners were gone.

Kenny's heart was bitter. 'I'll get von Wohl one of these days,' he muttered as he drew reluctantly away with the last to leave.

There was no attempt to attack them as they retreated.

It was hot. The sun beat down, and the dust rose from the rolling wheels and the mustang hoofs. The rear guard hung back in case von Wohl's killers tried to come up on them.

When they had left the vicinity of the rancho behind them, there was a short stop while the leaders conferred. Some suggested that they go to Soledad, but Kenny reminded them that Froleiks was there, and that von Wohl had control of the town.

'Let's go on, and find a place to camp,' he advised. 'When Don Joaquin's back with us, we'll decide what to do.'

They camped that night at the side of the road. Don Joaquin found them there, and told them that Mariano had a chance to live, provided he was not disturbed. The bleeding had been checked. He was being taken care of at the doctor's ranch, and his mother was with him.

The men sat up, talking, until late. Don Joaquin's courage had returned, with Mariano having a fighting chance.

'We mus' find a safe place where we can settle, *amigos mios*,' said Don Joaquin. 'Zere are some lands, not much account, ees true, but pairhaps we mak' zem so. I hav' a map.'

Next day, Kenny accompanied Don Joaquin and several other leaders on a ride to the east, toward the Cabilans. They reached a vast tableland, stretching for many miles, but with no trees. Only short grasses were growing there. The warm wind swept in their faces.

'Here, no one claims,' said Guiterrez. 'We may settle for a time, teel we know what nex' to do.'

'How about water?' asked Kenny.

He had dismounted, and was examining the dry soil, running it through his fingers.

'We try to deeg well,' said Don Joaquin.

'It's good dirt in which anything will grow, I believe,' said Kenny. 'Only there's no water.'

They had shovels, and began to dig. Kenny labored with the rest. They had dug through the soil to a depth of a dozen feet when magically the dry dirt became wet, water seeping through. Kenny strained a little, to taste it.

'It's fresh and cool!' he announced.

Men were sent back, to direct the caravan to the spot.

CHAPTER ELEVEN

SQUATTERS

Even more than for the tired Rio Kid it had been necessary for Saber to rest. Also Marshal Carmody had been in the last stages of exhaustion. The men had slept through the day and into the night after their meeting in Monterey with Leland Stanford, California's former governor.

In the morning, the Rio Kid and Carmody went to see about their horses which were at the livery stable. Carmody's horse was still lame, so he had to rent a mount. Pryor groomed Saber while Carmody chose an animal to ride.

They took the main highway out of Monterey, the road gently climbing from the amphitheater in which the town nestled. In the brilliant sunlight the blue bay, with the mighty Pacific beyond, glistened in loveliness.

They made good time on the beaten trail. Around noon they came to a wayside inn and there stood Leland Stanford's wagon outside, but the railroaders had gone off on horseback into the wilds. Pressed by the knowledge of the peril to those at the Guiterrez rancho, with von Wohl on the loose, Pryor and Carmody pushed on. The marshal was determined to atone for what he had done.

They rode with eyes sweeping the way ahead, aware of Manfred von Wohl's hostility, the danger of a dry-gulcher's slug. Travelers passing now and then greeted them with the polite *'Buenos dias'* of the countryside. The riders did not run into any of von Wohl's patrols.

Some rising dust approaching from the south sent them off to one side, to check up on who was coming. They waited until the two horsemen bobbed up over the rise.

'Celestino—Jo!' sang out the Rio Kid.

They were his comrades, Mireles and Jo Walker. At the sound of his partner's voice, Celestino rose high in his stirrups, uttering a shrill whoop of joy. He tore up to the Rio Kid, waving his sombrero, his brown face wreathed in smiles.

'General, ees you! *Compadre mio!'* He seized the Rio Kid's hand. 'What happen? I hunt, day and night. I geeve up, almos', and theenk you dead.'

Jo Walker arrived, grinning, and slapped Pryor on the back.

'Told 'em yuh'd show up, Rio Kid. We're mighty glad to find yuh. Looked in every haystack. For a while we thought von Wohl had yuh.'

Celestino's face was drawn, showing the strain he had been under. He had slept only in snatches since the night in Soledad when he had been unable to locate the Rio Kid.

'We look, all of us,' explained Mireles. 'We go look at von Wohl's. Zey fire at us, but zere was no sign zey had you. I try to follow Saber's tracks but zey are los' in town dust. Ees mystery.'

They rode together on the Salinas road and the Rio Kid explained how Sheriff Froleiks and von Wohl had used Marshal Carmody as a catspaw to rid themselves of their dangerous foe, the Rio Kid.

'Then they expected to ambush me'n Carmody easy enough on the road,' he said, 'but Carmody fooled 'em. When the showdown come he handed me my guns and we fought 'em off.' He changed the subject. 'What's up now? Is von Wohl still lyin' low? Froleiks showed me some legal papers that I reckon von Wohl forged. They called for seizure of the Guiterrez rancho.'

'Shucks!' Jo Walker swore and spat. 'That's so. We been so busy chewin' our tongues we forgot yuh didn't savvy. To put it in a nutshell, Guiterrez give up his ranch. Von Wohl's got it.'

'What!' The Rio Kid jumped in his saddle and rage flushed his face. 'How did that happen?'

'*Si, si.*' Mireles nodded. 'While we hunt you, von Wohl come to rancho weeth beeg gang. Zey throw bomb, zey wound Mariano.'

The sad tale came out. Celestino and Jo Walker had trailed the dispossessed people,

99

when they had ridden back for a brief respite, and had learned all that had occurred . . .

It was the following morning before the four men who had met on the road reached the nondescript camp where the erstwhile powerful Don Joaquin Guiterrez squatted with his friends, the Californios. Canvas tarpaulins had been stretched, and they had brought brush and limbs from the wilds to make shelters for women and children.

They had saved little when they had been forced to flee from von Wohl's forces. They were sharing what they had, living as a community, cooking game shot by vaqueros in the mountains, or beefs they could find strayed from their own ranges. They had some bags of flour, salt, sugar, coffee, frijoles, and other necessities.

They welcomed the return of the Rio Kid, smiling, shaking his hand. They were gay enough in spite of adversity. Don Joaquin was there, but Donna Ysabel was still with the wounded Mariano. Each night Guiterrez rode to see how his son and wife fared.

* * *

The Rio Kid tended Saber and turned the dun loose to graze. Then he looked around the camp. It stood near the margins of the great tableland, and according to Don Joaquin's maps, no one had ever bothered to claim the

100

section, since there was no water available. No streams cut through for many miles, and there were no woods to break the brown-green monotony.

Dave Kenny was delighted to see the Rio Kid. And unlike the majority in the camp, Kenny was interested in the bare expanse here.

'It's fine soil,' he insisted, as he stood with Pryor, staring out at the plateau. 'It'll grow anything. I've ridden around some, testing the dirt, and wheat'll do fine here—wheat or truck crops, whatever you wish to plant. If there was only water! You know what? I've been down and put in a claim for a section allowed a war veteran, and I mean to figure out a way to farm here.'

'Water?' said the Rio Kid. 'Yuh got a well there, I see. Tastes mighty sweet.'

'Yes, we struck some spring at the edge. Only a dozen feet down.'

The Rio Kid scratched his head. The aspect of the plateau did not intrigue him, because it was too bare. And he recalled how thirsty Carmody and he had grown when crossing it, how the horses had suffered.

'Any of the others file on sections here?' he inquired.

'No. They've been too busy keepin' body and soul together, and most of them are hopin' to find a better place to settle. But all the good land in the valley is in use.'

Cattle could not be run without plenty of

water for them. Truck farming, too, required irrigation ditches, at least. Water would have to be bought or perhaps piped from the distant mountains, if this place was to be made usable.

The Rio Kid learned that Kenny, who acted as Don Joaquin's field general, insisted on keeping a day and night guard out, to watch for von Wohl. But so far they had not been molested. Vaqueros sent to spy on the Prussian from a distance reported that von Wohl was living on the great Guiterrez rancho, with his gang. And from Soledad came reports that von Wohl and Froleiks were seizing political control.

'He's ambitious, this von Wohl skunk,' said Kenny. 'I understand he is planning on running high in politics, perhaps governor some day. The way he gets what he wants, he may make it. They say he's taking on more and more helpers, toughs from the mines and riffraff from the ranges.'

Such a gang might well control elections, the Rio Kid knew. And von Wohl counted on the human failing of indifference to the troubles of others by the general public, of those who were not yet touched by his grasping claws.

Thinking, trying to marshal his powers against von Wohl, to find some way to check the Prussian's seizure of the Salinas lands, the Rio Kid the next morning rode to Soledad with ten picked men. Mireles, Jo Walker, the

Castros and half a dozen other young vaqueros were in the party. Marshal Ben Carmody also went along.

There was a bustle in the usually quiet town. In front of the *Cantina Royale* stood Leland Stanford's fancy rig. Gaping brown children stared at the elegant equipage and fine horses. In the dining room, Stanford, Huntington and the engineers were having breakfast preparatory to setting out.

Sheriff Froleiks was not about. Signs proclaiming Manfred von Wohl for commissioner covered the town walls. Leaving his friends to keep a sharp lookout on the highways, in case von Wohl's gang should appear, the Rio Kid went in and greeted Stanford and his companions.

Stanford was cordial with him.

'Sit down and have coffee and a bite, Rio Kid,' he invited, and summoned a Mexican youth to take the order.

Bob Pryor pulled up a chair and exchanged the usual greetings with Stanford and his party. Huntington stared rather coolly, as he gave a short nod, and Pryor felt that Stanford himself was uneasy.

'Von Wohl did, it, Guv'nor!' he said. 'He ran Don Joaquin Guiterrez off his ranch with guns and forged papers. Now von Wohl's in control.'

'Yes, yes.' Stanford nodded. 'That's so. I had a talk with von Wohl last evening, after we arrived. But when I asked him about the charges you'd made, he denied them.'

* * *

Although Stanford himself was friendly enough, the atmosphere was frosty.

'I didn't expect von Wohl to admit he was a killer and thief,' drawled the Rio Kid.

'He has a lot of influence in this section,' remarked Huntington. 'It's not our business to interfere in local politics. We've got enough worries as it is.'

'Yuh're buildin' yore depot near here?' asked the Rio Kid.

'Yes. It'll clear the Salinas Valley produce.'

'That means plenty for von Wohl, now that he's seized everything in sight by fair means and foul, chiefly foul! Gents, I savvy how yuh're fixed. Yuh got to consider business.'

'That's right.' Huntington nodded. He had a legal mind, and it was he who handled the railroad affairs in Washington. 'There are proper authorities to complain to, sir, in case you have charges to lodge. We have a great deal of money involved, and we must think of our investors as well as of our own pockets.'

The Rio Kid drew a map of the region from his pocket, and spread it out before Stanford.

'Here's somethin' I'm thinkin' of, Guv'nor. Yuh see this big blank space, east of the valley? It's a great plateau, bare except for

104

grasses. Guiterrez and others are buildin' a settlement there and either ranchin' or farmin' on it. How about it? A branch line in from yore main road would be easy to lay.'

It was a hunch the Rio Kid had had. A railroad increased land values tremendously, and he had hoped to salvage something for the victims of the Prussian's greed. He waited eagerly for an opinion from these hard-headed far-seeing men who were bringing changes to the West.

Stanford glanced at his engineers.

'What about it, Rawson?'

General Rawson put on his spectacles. He had a master map of the region, including the tableland the Rio Kid pointed out. It was more accurate and detailed than Pryor's own map, which had been obtained from Don Joaquin.

'But there's no water, not even a spring, on the entire expanse,' said Rawson, after he had studied his key chart.

'It's absurd,' growled Huntington. 'Young man, do you know what it would cost us to build a spur to that region?'

'Now, Rio Kid, you're a friend and I'll do anything I can for you,' Stanford said, smiling. 'If you want a position, all you have to do is to ask, and I'll put you on as a guard or a surveyor's helper, anything you fancy. You can have a foreman's job if you like. But you must understand we can't run a branch line to any place because a friend asks us to. I couldn't do it, even if I wished, without my partners' permission. A railroad has to be built where people have settled, or at least where they may be expected to settle. And no one in his right mind will build a home and try to farm or ranch without water.'

'As a matter of fact,' said Huntington, 'we might be willing to oblige you, Rio Kid, if this section had any favorable aspects, for von Wohl is trying to hold us up for a larger price than we wish to pay for his land. But we would be fools to run such a barren route.'

Shrewd, first-class businessmen, Stanford, Huntington and Hopkins were controlled by economic factors.

'Forget it, gents.' The Rio Kid smiled, putting away his map. 'We'll get along somehow.'

He ate a meal with them. They were smoking their cigars, preparatory to riding out again, when he took his leave.

CHAPTER TWELVE

NEW START

With Dave Kenny and Carmody in tow, the Rio Kid, Jo Walker and Celestino moved across the grassy tableland. It was the following day, after Pryor's talk in Soledad with Stanford. They carried picks and small shovels, and now and again the Rio Kid stopped to have Kenny examine the soil.

'Good stuff—It'll grow anything.' That was Kenny's unfailing report. 'Only it needs water.'

'I got an idea of irrigatin', somehow, from the Cabilans, mebbe,' said the Rio Kid.

It persisted in his mind; and he could not let it go, this fancy for the huge plateau. Here was good land, already cleared, without even high grasses and the wild mustard of the Santa Lucia slopes. There were few rocks, no gullies to speak of. A plough could be run straight and with speed.

It was hot, even with the breeze which blew unimpeded over the high flats. They were near the center of the tableland at noon when they stopped, under the blazing sun, to eat iron rations and gulp a few swigs from their canteens.

The horses were thirsty. Saber, the dun, was pawing at the ground. He kept snorting, rippling the black stripe down his spine, shaking his mane. Then he would resume his scratching of the soil. The other animals, too, sniffed and dug in with their hoofs.

'That was a mighty dry ride we took across here,' remarked Carmody to the Rio Kid who was lying on one elbow as he smoked a cigarette after the meal, idly watching the horses. Then suddenly Saber's antics began to have meaning.

'Now, I wonder,' Carmody murmured.

He rose, went and got his shovel and pick, and began digging into the fine loam.

Kenny grew interested, and joined him. Soon the five were at it, throwing up spadefuls of dirt.

'It's good all the way down!' exclaimed the sweating Kenny, who was deeply interested in farming.

The Rio Kid, up to his waist in the hole they had dug, kept at it. His head was about a foot below the surface when his shovel end broke through a thin crust and came out wet. Then the crust was weakened by the break, and his legs went suddenly down through the cracking earth and he was up to his waist in cold water. He saved himself from slipping further by throwing out his arms and holding to the sides. Mireles, in the hole with him, gripped the edge of the pit. Carmody, Kenny and Walker craned their necks, gaping down at them.

A lasso helped them out. The Rio Kid tied a

rock to one end of the rope, and lowered it through the break. When he withdrew it, the rope was wet halfway up its length.

'It's fifteen, twenty feet deep, boys!' the Rio Kid cried.

When they tasted the water, they found it cool and sweet. They brought up what they could in their hats and let the horses refresh themselves.

'C'mon, let's get goin'!' The Rio Kid was excited.

A half-mile to the north he pulled up, and they dug another well, hitting water at eleven feet. Their hands were callused from the use of lariat and leather, and general hard work, but digging took a different set of muscles and their arms ached from the unaccustomed toil. However, before dark fell, they had sunk half a dozen wells, and every one had struck the same cool, deep water.

'Our hunch is right, I'm shore!' declared the Rio Kid. 'There's a big underground lake under this whole plateau. Yuh hit it wherever yuh dig.'

Dave Kenny's breath came fast, and it wasn't all from digging.

'By hook, you're right! The water we need to farm with is right underneath our feet!'

'Yuh can tap it with pumps or windmills,' said the Rio Kid. 'There's steady breezes here most of the day. I reckon the water is drainage from the mountains to the east. It runs under

109

the earth and is held down by contours and mebbe that thin crust.'

'Why,' exclaimed Ben Carmody, 'this land is worth a fortune!'

'I wonder what Leland Stanford will have to say now,' drawled the Rio Kid. 'But I reckon we won't be letting him and his bunch know anything about it until we're good and ready . . .'

Two weeks passed after the Rio Kid and his friends discovered that the plateau was over a great water table. The days went swiftly, for there was much to do. The first thing the Rio Kid insisted on was that Guiterrez, the Castros and others file legal claims on the land. He meant to see they had a new start in life. No one had ever owned or laid claim to the apparently barren district, and their tides would be entirely clear.

They saw to it that all Government requirements were fulfilled. Each claimant started a building, turned the soil. Water was no problem, for all a man needed to do was dig a dozen feet to hit an inexhaustible well.

*　　　*　　　*

Not until they had all the sections filed on did the Rio Kid again call on Leland Stanford. He had told his story, and returned, and now he was expecting the former state executive to appear. But it was Jo Walker who first spied the railroad man.

'Here comes Leland Stanford and his bunch, Rio Kid!' called Walker, who had been on the lookout, and all eyes were on the approaching equipage.

Stanford, with Huntington and Rawson, the chief engineer on the new railroad project, drove up to the main camp of the settlers. The Rio Kid kept a force of riders ready there, in case of trouble, though lately they had heard little of von Wohl.

They had kept away from Soledad, and from the former Guiterrez property. The Rio Kid had been too rushed to deal with his arch-enemy, but he meant to crush von Wohl when the right time came. Aware of von Wohl's greediness, his ruthless determination to be boss of the Salinas, the Rio Kid was making plans.

Dave Kenny was out on the section he had filed on. He was building a windmill, laying out his fields, determining what crops he would start with. He so loved the earth and its fruits that he was completely enthralled with the new country.

Leland Stanford was all smiles, as he shook hands with the Rio Kid. Huntington, too, seemed less reserved.

'We'd like to talk to you, Rio Kid,' said Stanford. 'Suppose we sit here in the shade of the carriage top?'

Those in camp stared at the railroad men as

the Rio Kid climbed into the fine vehicle, taking the driver's seat. He accepted a bottle which Huntington proffered.

'I'm going to lay all the cards on the table,' began Stanford at once. 'Since you last got in touch with me, Rawson and his men have made an exhaustive survey of this tableland. There's a vast underground lake under the entire district, as you suspected. Evidently it is drainage from the hills. Analysis of the water shows it to be pure and without calcium or magnesium salts, or other deleterious impurities.'

'An important point,' said Rawson. 'A good deal of the natural waters we run into can't be used in locomotive boilers. They cake the metal and clog the pipes with precipitates.'

'We're willing to come through this way with our railroad, provided you're reasonable,' continued Stanford. 'We believe this district will be well populated as soon as the truth about the water situation becomes known.'

'Von Wohl's trying to hold us up,' Huntington put in. 'He's asking crazy prices for the land we need. It's farther around this way, but we might build on the route. We need sites for our shops and for a station.'

The Rio Kid had his answer ready.

'Gents, yuh don't need to worry about price on the land yuh'll need. I've filed on a central section and I'm willin' to give the lots yuh want to the railroad for a station and shops. It'll

112

make the rest of the section worth plenty, and help the whole neighborhood. And I don't need to tell yuh I'll be glad to see von Wohl left holdin' the bag!'

The railroad would run along the western edge of the great tableland. A station would be built, and around it the settlers would erect their town. Produce would flow to the freight cars, produce from farms and small ranches, and dairy establishments. It would feed north, to Monterey and San Francisco and other cities.

Von Wohl, believing he had the railroad people where he wanted them, had over-reached himself. He had demanded too high a price for land needed, and the railroad men would avoid the properties he had stolen.

When Stanford and his party had driven off, the Rio Kid turned to his friends, grinning with delight.

'Wait'll von Wohl hears the railroad ain't comin' through the land he's stole! Stanford and Huntington'll soon let him savvy.'

'He'll hit the sky!' Jo Walker nodded.

Celestino Mireles was pleased, too, but worried. 'He weel attack, General,' he told the Rio Kid. 'We must be ready.'

'*Si*,' agreed Pryor. 'I figger he'll think of somethin' to make a bad ruckus, but this time we'll be watchin' for him.'

The Rio Kid had picked fifteen young fighting men, from among the Californians.

Carmody, Mireles, the Castros, Kenny and others, as well as old Jo Walker who was as good if not better than the usual run of scrapper, would be armed and on hand day or night.

*   *   *

Don Joaquin was busy, between his new land and the home of the physician where Mariano lay, recovering from the wound dealt him by von Wohl. Structures had been raised on the claims, tents, and cartloads of baked adobe bricks were coming in as houses were hastily erected. Horses and cattle were being collected.

There were a million things to do, but the Rio Kid never relaxed his guard. He knew von Wohl's nature, knew that when the Prussian realized he had been defeated, and that his former victims were rising to new heights of prosperity at his expense, von Wohl would strike.

Stanford's surveyors were already on the tableland. They were pushing their transits rapidly across the level earth, staking the route.

They were in camp one morning when the first alarm came in. It was a message from Dave Kenny, who was out at his farm. He had sent a lad, Feliciano, one of Don Joaquin's nephews, to the Rio Kid. The note read:

Six squatters just drove up in a wagon and unloaded a portable house on western section of my land. They look like von Wohl men.

'Here we go, boys,' said the Rio Kid. 'Von Wohl's on the prowl agin.'

He quickly called his forces together. Marshal Carmody, Mireles, Walker and ten more men, ready and waiting, were armed and mounted within minutes, and following the Rio Kid across the flats.

'He's learned that Stanford's comin' thisaway,' said the Rio Kid, 'and he's tryin' to horn in on the party!'

They rapidly covered the several miles to the spot which Kenny had indicated. Near it, they could see the rising frame of Kenny's windmill in the distance and Kenny himself rode toward them.

'They're over there,' said Dave. 'I waited for you boys, like you told me to,'

'*Bueno*,' said the Rio Kid. 'Let's go.'

CHAPTER THIRTEEN

THE MEETING

Drawn up in a hollow stood a flat wagon and the horses of the squatters. They had brought in a small portable house, only a shell made of light wood with a window hole cut in one end and a doorless entry. It was the old game of rushing in and getting up some sort of structure so as to validate a claim. They also had brought plenty of whisky and bags of provisions.

Their leader, who hastily seized his rifle when he saw the vaqueros coming, was a square-set, bearded fellow whom the Rio Kid remembered having seen at von Wohl's. The rest were heavily armed, toughs who rode for the Prussian.

'Hold up there,' the bearded leader yelled. 'Stay where yuh are! What yuh want?'

'Yuh're squattin' on staked land, Whiskers,' replied the Rio Kid. 'It's all signed and sealed in Dave Kenny's name. Fact is, the whole plateau is under legal claim by different parties. You go on back and tell that to von Wohl.'

'We ain't movin'!' growled 'Whiskers'. 'We got a buildin' up and we aim to stick.'

'Well, we'll compromise,' said the Rio Kid,

winking at Mireles and Walker, who flanked him. 'Yuh can each have six feet by two of ground. Yuh ought to make good fertilizer.'

The squatters were nervous. They had no cover, save for the wagon, and the Rio Kid's patrol outnumbered them two to one.

Whiskers conferred with his friends. They stood in defensive attitudes.

'I'll count to ten!' called the Rio Kid. 'If yuh ain't started by that time, we're comin' in and shove yuh off!'

He began the slow count.

'One—two—three—'

He had reached 'Six' when a slight gunny behind Whiskers turned and began throwing cases into the wagon. Another joined him at the count of 'Seven,' and at 'Nine' Whiskers himself hastily turned and began packing up.

Guns up, the Rio Kid slowly moved in. The squatters were in the wagon and on horses, and they hit the faint trail west by which they had come. The Rio Kid fired over them, whooping derisively. Mireles and the others joined in with catcalls and jibes, as von Wohl's party hurried away, leaving the six-by-six house frame.

'It'll make good firewood,' said Jo Walker.

Next day Don Joaquin called for help. Several more squatters had appeared, on his claim, and the Rio Kid hurried to the spot with his patrol. They were on the line surveyed by the railroad, and there were a dozen of them.

As the Rio Kid hailed them, he recognized several von Wohl followers in the crew. 'Yuh're on staked land, boys. *Vamose!*' They argued, parleyed for a time. The Rio Kid, his fighting men ready and numbering fifteen this time, opened fire with rifles, but the Rio Kid had ordered it high. At sound of the singing bullets, the von Wohl claim-jumpers hastily packed up their belongings and fled.

'Now what's his idea in sendin' these parties in?' growled the Rio Kid, as he watched the enemy in full retreat toward the road to Soledad. 'Yuh reckon he aims to establish some sort of legal claim thisaway?'

'*Si*, perhaps,' said Celestino, nodding. 'Can he not say we drive *hees amigos* off by force?'

'I aim to find out what he's up to,' said Bob Pryor. 'This evenin' I'm goin' to look over von Wohl's . . .'

From the hilltop, just before dark, the Rio Kid observed von Wohl's stronghold, the Guiterrez rancho. Walker, Mireles, Carmody, Kenny and the Castros were with him.

'There goes von Wohl,' announced the Rio Kid. 'He's got forty gunnies with him. Looks like they're headed for town.'

The Prussian, with his heavily armed retainers, rode toward Soledad in the dying light. Pryor did not see Hans, the giant German.

'He's in charge of the rancho guards,' he

decided. 'Let's foller and see what holds.'

The road was clear, and night had come as they followed von Wohl. Risen dust from the beating hoofs of the Prussian's mustangs hung in the warm air.

The Rio Kid held back so as not to alarm his enemies. But as they reached Soledad, he saw them framed against the settlement's yellow glow, when von Wohl led his men in to town.

* * *

The Rio Kid soon discovered why von Wohl had come to Soledad that evening. Filtering through town, keeping to the side ways, they came upon a printed announcement that read:

MEETING THURSDAY NIGHT 8 PM HEAR MANFRED VON WOHL, OUR NEXT COMMISSIONER!

'So that's it,' said the Rio Kid, as his force of men gathered about him against the board fence where the sign was tacked. 'Von Wohl's goin' to make a speech tonight. Shore enough, the town hall's lit up! I reckon I'll listen to what von Wohl has to say.'

'Be careful,' warned Carmody. 'They got a mighty tough bunch with 'em tonight, Rio Kid. They'll shoot yuh first and ask questions afterward. But I'm with yuh, whatever yuh do.'

'I ain't goin' to walk right in with the crowd,' said the Rio Kid. 'No doubt von Wohl's bodyguard'll be near. But we'll see what's what.'

There was no doubt in the Rio Kid's mind that von Wohl was furious over the turn of affairs concerning the railroad. And the Prussian, greedy for wealth as well as power, must be planning a way to destroy Guiterrez, Kenny, and the rest of the lucky ones who had filed claims on the tableland. They would be a menace to him, always, a nucleus of opposition which might grow and destroy him. In the public eye as a politician, von Wohl must maintain a respectable front.

The schoolhouse, which was also used as a town hall and meeting place, stood at the other side of the plaza from Froleiks' office and the jail. It was built in mission style, of baked brown adobe brick, and there was a cupola with a brass bell in it topping the roof.

It was nearly eight o'clock. Someone was slowly pulling the long rope which made the bell toll calling the public to the assembly.

Von Wohl and his crew had paused at *El Cantina Royale* to wet their whistles. A good many citizens from the range had flocked in to the settlement, for such political meetings formed a basic source of entertainment for the public. Colorful costumes of Old Mexico, graceful vaqueros, and dons in serapes, velvet, and high steeple sombreros could be seen among the more soberly clad Anglo-Saxons in leather or whipcord trousers, high boots, and Stetsons.

Some were farmers, some ranchers, some in trade. So far, von Wohl had attacked only a handful of families, all of them rancheros such as Castro and Guiterrez. He had chosen the lands which had been along the tentative route laid out on Leland Stanford's maps for his railroad. Otherwise the Prussian had kept his reputation fairly clean, for he must have votes, the support of the public.

The Prussian could have his henchmen vote, several times per man, perhaps, and intimidate some into casting their ballots, but in the long run any candidate with aspirations must have a general following. For this reason, as well as to protect himself from the law, von Wohl always used a pretense of legality in dispossessing his victims.

Carriages were driving up, and there were women in the audience. Men, after seeing that the women were seated, would hustle out for a quick drink at one of the saloons before the meeting began. There was an excited, pleasant bustle all around the schoolhouse.

Lines of trees had been planted in the surrounding yard and a huge live-oak with branches spreading close to the ground grew at the rear corner of the place.

'We'll make that live-oak, boys,' said the Rio Kid, after a look-see. 'Pastor, you hold the hosses here in the shadows behind the fence. Keep 'em quiet.'

Pastor Castro's arm had healed, though it was still stiff. The others, following the Rio Kid's instructions, began flitting toward the live-oak, whose low-spreading branches would offer concealment.

But von Wohl did not believe his foes would dare beard him in the lighted town, which he controlled through Froleiks. He had brought a large number of fighters along, but chiefly to act as a claque, truckling applauders of his words.

It was a hot night, and the schoolhouse windows were wide open. The benches and desks were filled, and extra seats had been brought in. Men lined both walls and stood in the rear. Oil lamps hung from the rafters where insects flirted with the deadly flames. A pleasant confusion of talk was in the air. Friends and neighbors exchanged greetings, calling and waving to one another.

* * *

Manfred Von Wohl, clad in a brushed, dark suit, a white shirt with a black stringtie and highly polished boots, walked around, shaking hands. He gave his foreign bow from the hips as he sought to ingratiate himself with the ladies and gentlemen who would soon cast their votes in the coming election. A smile was frozen on von Wohl's usually cold lips. His stiff flaxen hair was clipped short and well-brushed. He had recently waxed his bristling mustache.

Sheriff Froleiks was on hand, a cud of tobacco in his leathery cheek. He had changed his shirt for the momentous occasion and shaved off his straggly whiskers. He stood by the entrance, checking those who came in.

There was a foot-high platform at the other end of the schoolroom, a place where the teacher could sit and watch over the vagaries of pupils. This was used as a rostrum, and when von Wohl had finished the handshaking, he went around to the small side door which led him directly in to the platform, and took his seat.

The side door was left open, for it was warm, with the packed crowd and the burning lamps.

Applause greeted Sheriff Froleiks as the lawman stood on the platform to introduce the principal speaker, Manfred von Wohl. All eyes were on the show, as the Rio Kid flitted over and stood at an open window, to one side, where he could hear without being observed by those inside.

'And now, folks,' Sheriff Froleiks was saying, 'I introduce Manfred von Wohl, the people's candidate for commissioner. Yuh all savvy him. He's an up and comin' hombre. He ain't been in the Salinas Valley long but he's made a name for hisself as a square dealer, a feller

123

who has the real good of the people at heart—Mr. von Wohl.'

The Prussian was smiling as he acknowledged the applause. His followers stamped, whistled, banged their heels on the desks, cheered, and the contagion spread. When they had subsided somewhat, von Wohl raised his hand and began to speak:

'Ladies and gentlemen: This is a splendid gathering. I can see you are the salt of our country, the real aristocracy of Salinas. You have made this land what it is and you deserve to enjoy its fruits. You, rather than the handful of grasping men who have jealously held it against you.

'Tonight I am going to speak straight from the shoulder. I am going to name names, and not mince matters, for I am an honest, straightforward person. Because I have fought against injustice, lies have been spread against me by those I oppose. Chief among these is Joaquin Guiterrez.

'This man has led a faction which has flouted the law, as Sheriff Froleiks and others will testify. I would like to see him and his kind driven from Salinas, from California, from the United States. They are not Americans, they are foreign to us. Are they not?

'Guiterrez, Castro, and such scum deserve no consideration. They have forfeited all rights to such. They have fired on legally sworn-in posses seeking only to carry out the edicts of our courts. They have killed and stolen.'

Von Wohl was working himself up to a pitch of fury, and his voice became shriller as he attacked Guiterrez and the rest of the Californios who had opposed him.

'Where is this Guiterrez now, with his slimy ways? He has seized a huge new empire, and flagrantly thrust out those who had first settled upon it! I have friends who can testify that Guiterrez hired ruffians, one in particular known in outlaw circles as the Rio Kid, to terrorize this district. Yes, this Rio Kid and his master, Guiterrez, who pays him, have gunned decent American citizens, chased them off the lands they occupied!'

Von Wohl's lies had a tissue of fact. There were the squatters he had sent, to seize parts of the coveted plateau, men whom the Rio Kid had run off.

'Now I savvy why he had 'em come in thataway,' Bob Pryor thought grimly.

CHAPTER FOURTEEN

SPEECH

Von Wohl had a savage tongue, as he went on flaying the Californios. He was playing on race prejudice, and the scattering of Mexicans looked about them uneasily as von Wohl excoriated Guiterrez. Several stood up to leave the assembly, but instantly von Wohl's toughs were upon them, forcing them to remain.

'Why should we stand for such people in our midst?' shrieked von Wohl, banging the desk with his fist. 'Why don't we go, now, and ride them on a rail out of our country? They are the scum of the earth!'

The poison spewed by von Wohl had its effect. The listening people, drinking it in, could not help but be affected, decided the Rio Kid, unless an antidote were quickly administered. Von Wohl's fabrications, his vicious lying, could start a race war which would sweep through southern California, and do irreparable harm.

An answering fury rose in the Rio Kid's bold heart at the challenge to mankind.

'I'll show him up, here and now!' he muttered.

He hurried back to the big live-oak, where his aides were sheltered, and gave his orders.

126

Celestino was appalled. He sought to dissuade the Rio Kid. It was too dangerous, he said. The von Wohl faction would kill him there in the lighted hall.

But the Rio Kid was determined, set on choking off von Wohl's screaming, savage voice. For once started, von Wohl, ambitious for political office, might keep on to dizzy heights.

It took but a few minutes for Carmody, Celestino, Jo Walker, Dave Kenny and Ygnacio Castro to get in position, shotguns or carbines ready, outside the windows. The Rio Kid went swiftly through the side door which led directly to the rostrum, and leaped up beside Manfred von Wohl.

'Hey, you!'

That was Froleiks, on von Wohl's other side, as the startled sheriff recognized the intruder.

'Dry up, Froleiks!' snapped Pryor. 'Set down and keep quiet!'

Von Wohl's voice died off in a squeak. He was astounded, and could scarcely believe his eyes as he saw the Rio Kid just at his elbow.

'Stand where yuh are, von Wohl, or I'll drill yuh,' threatened the Rio Kid, in the Prussian's ear.

He took care to keep slightly to the rear of his enemy, so that he was shielded by the German's bulk as well as by the desk.

Von Wohl's face was crimson, from his shouting, from the heat of the hall. His up-pointed mustache trembled, and his breath came fast. A yellow fear came into his eyes, but he dared not budge.

The entrance of the Rio Kid had stunned the audience for a moment. Silence was upon the gathering when Carmody's clear voice spoke up:

'Set down, boys. Stay where yuh are and yuh won't get hurt. I'm Federal Marshal Ben Carmody from Sacramento, and I'm with the Rio Kid. He's a decent, honest hombre, and von Wohl's a killer and thief!'

Several of von Wohl's gunnies, who had started to sneak out the main door, meaning to get around and down Pryor, sensibly resumed their seats. They could see the gunbarrels at the various windows.

'You folks needn't be afraid of bein' hurt,' began the Rio Kid. 'I'm here just to talk to yuh. I've been listenin' to what von Wohl has said, and I never heard a worse pack of lies! They're dangerous lies, too, the sort that rouse good folks against each other. Joaquin Guiterrez is a fine citizen, a man of decent life, and von Wohl has cheated him, forged notes and mortgages, and stole his ranch from him, just the way he did with Felipe Castro. He killed Castro, in cold blood!

'Von Wohl is tryin' to set yuh against Guiterrez and his people. Don't let him succeed. Von Wohl's a schemer, he means to own the Salinas, mebbe more and more of the state as he gains his power. The men he spoke of came and squatted on the new lands, to which Guiterrez and his friends were driven, when von Wohl stole his property, and wounded Mariano, his son.'

The Rio Kid paused. He had spoken with a tense conviction, driving home his points, condemning Manfred von Wohl. The listeners heard him, impressed by his earnestness, by the clearness of his voice, the manliness of his looks.

'I got no axe to grind in these parts, folks,' he went on. 'I came here to help the kinfolks and friends of my pardner, Celestino Mireles. It's been a hard fight, for von Wohl is strong, he's ruthless, and he will kill to get what he wants. If yuh need to ride somebody on a rail out of the valley, make it von Wohl, and save yourselves. For if yuh let him grow much stronger, he'll be yore master. The big thing is to live in peace with yore neighbors, and Guiterrez and his kind are yore friends, Americans like all of us.'

*   *   *

Von Wohl was shaking with mingled rage and fright. He knew the Rio Kid's speed, the desperate assurance of the man in a fight.

The Rio Kid gripped the Prussian's arm.

'Tell 'em yuh lied, von Wohl! Yuh lied when yuh said Guiterrez was a thief and cheat!'

129

Von Wohl's glaring, bulbous eyes met his in silent challenge.

The Rio Kid's fingers vised upon his arm.

'Tell 'em, von Wohl!'

The pale-blue eyes flickered. Von Wohl's face grew pale.

'I—I lied!' he said thickly.

Before the eyes of the audience he had showed the craven streak. A young woman in the back of the hall laughed nervously, then sudden laughter seized the gathering. They were laughing at von Wohl, whose knees had turned to water as he faced his nemesis, the Rio Kid.

The high moment had come, and the Rio Kid, aware of it, knew it was time to leave.

'Don't forget, folks!' he sang out. 'Vote for Guiterrez!'

'I'll vote for the Rio Kid!' shouted an enthusiast up front. 'Dog me if I ever seen a play like it in my life!'

The iron nerve of the Rio Kid, bearding von Wohl and his armed followers, seized on their imagination. Someone began to applaud as Pryor, Colt ready, backed to the side door and jumped outside.

He heard the rising bedlam in the meeting house, as he ran for the live-oak, his friends with him. Von Wohl's men would be after them, hunting them, thirsting to kill.

Jo Walker, Mireles, Kenny, all were laughing, laughing at von Wohl, at the success of the Rio Kid's act.

They raced to the spot where Pastor held the horses. Across the plaza, von Wohl's killers already were spreading out, guns up, looking for the interlopers. The crowd was streaming out of the schoolhouse. Whoops and catcalls rang out, as von Wohl emerged. Parties were hurrying to the saloons, to drink up and talk over the spectacular meeting.

Marshal Carmody couldn't stop chuckling. He wiped tears of joy from his eyes.

'I've seen plenty around the capitol, fellers, but that beats all! I can guarantee one thing, Rio Kid. Yuh shore nipped von Wohl's chances as a politician in the bud. This'll be all over the state by tomorrer. It's too good to miss. It'll be in all the papers.'

They rode out of Soledad and cut around, meaning to reach the route for home. Riders, followers of Froleiks and von Wohl, were spreading further out to hunt the hated Rio Kid. But Pryor and his friends cleared the settlement, moving off.

The Rio Kid was quiet. He was thinking. Perhaps it was true, he mused, that he had wrecked von Wohl's political aspirations by making a fool of him publicly, forcing him to show his yellow streak. Support might be withdrawn from von Wohl, by astute and venal politicians. But von Wohl was not yet beaten, by any means, for his wealth and power were increasing.

131

'He'll hit back and pronto,' he decided. 'And he'll be mad enough to kill every enemy he sights. I've got to check him.'

After a short run, he said:

'Boys, we ain't goin' home—not me, anyway. Ygnacio, I wish Pastor and you would ride like all get-out, though, and take a message to Don Joaquin. I want him to bring all the vaqueros he can gather up, on the double.'

'*Si, si*,' the Castros nodded, obedient to the Rio Kid's wishes. 'We go now, Rio Keed?'

'In a jiffy. Wait'll I give yuh an idea of what I aim to do. We got to strike von Wohl, before he comes after us.'

He gave them a sketch of his plan, elastic so that he might change details if need be. It was clear and bold, calling for the utmost courage and accurate timing.

The Castros rode off on fast horses, heading for the tableland and Don Joaquin, to call the vaqueros into action. The Rio Kid, with Mireles, Walker, Kenny, and Carmody circled around the town, and watched for any signs of the gunnies who were hunting them.

The settlement had quieted somewhat. People were leaving for home, after the exciting political rally in which they had seen the proud von Wohl abased by the Rio Kid. There were lights in Froleiks' quarters. Now and then a horseman would loom against the glow of the lamps.

'Dave,' the Rio Kid said to Kenny, 'I wish

132

Carmody and you would watch the hosses and keep 'em quiet. Walker, Mireles and I are goin' to sneak in and see what's up. Von Wohl'll be bilin' in his own juice tonight.'

*   *   *

It was necessary to leave the mustangs well out from the buildings to avoid detection. Bandannas were used to muzzle the animals, and the Rio Kid, with old Jo Walker and Celestino, made ready. Trained scouts, they discarded anything that would rattle, such as a cartridge belt or loose objects in the pockets. They put on moccasins, carried in their saddle-bags to be used when necessary to replace riding boots. Dirt cut the shine of their skin as they smudged their hands and faces.

'If yuh hear me whistlin,' "said the Big Black Charger to the Little White Mare," come tearin' in with the hosses,' warned the Rio Kid. 'It'll mean we've been spotted, boys.'

The tune he mentioned was an old Army favorite and Saber, the dun, knew the music and would run to it when he heard Bob Pryor whistle it.

The trio started flitting toward Soledad's plaza. Walker and Mireles were expert scouts and, with about twenty-five yards separating them, they moved in, taking advantage of every bush or rock or contour which would hide them. Reaching the first houses, they had

133

to be extremely careful not to bump into any of von Wohl's searchers, as they snaked through.

The Rio Kid checked, then hurried across the road to the line of trees at the plaza rim. Walker and Mireles made it.

The Rio Kid began to crawl as he neared the jail. He could see the open rear window, and hoped to discover what von Wohl and Froleiks were up to. Such work came naturally to him, and he had done a great deal of scouting for Custer and Sheridan during the Civil War.

Since then, he had sharpened his abilities on the Frontier, against Indians and against worse white renegades.

Stealthy as a hunting panther, the Rio Kid neared the jail.

Von Wohl, disgruntled, burning in his rage against the Rio Kid, was in there with his crony and aide, Sheriff Froleiks. A bottle of whisky had loosened the Prussian's tongue, made his voice louder, harsher.

'He has ruined my chances,' von Wohl repeated, again and again.

Froleiks sought to calm his master down.

'Aw, they'll soon fergit it, boss.'

'No. Only with the Rio Kid's death will my honor be absolved. We will say I bested him in a man-to-man duel, when I bring in his hide.' Von Wohl consulted the bottle again. His eyes bulged, his mustache gleamed with drops of liquor. 'We must, we will attack! What use now to worry what the world may say? Anyway, we will have plenty of witnesses on our side, and leave none to testify against us. I will take hostages, women and children, and threaten to torture them if Guiterrez and his gang won't surrender! They are spread out over the new district, so it should be simple to destroy them, one by one.'

'Yuh aim to start tonight?' asked Froleiks.

'No. I am tired, I need sleep. My nerves are ragged from the shame of what happened at the meeting, my friend. Besides, I must finish the necessary papers, in order to make my claim on the new lands. I'll block Stanford, force him to pay me what I ask. He won't be able to come into the Salinas without my say-so. And I want you to collect some more fighters, so there will be no mistakes.'

'I'll have to head over to Dinny's Roost if yuh want many more, von Wohl,' said the sheriff. 'A bunch just come in there from the mines, I hear—mebbe thirty, forty good men.'

'Very well, hire them, on a weekly basis. We can drop them as soon as the job's done. As for me, I will go to the hotel and take a room. I must have sleep. There's a young lady, too, waiting to have supper with me there. I will leave early in the morning for the hacienda. You pick up the men at Dinny's.'

'All right,' said the sheriff. 'I'll take 'em direct to yore place.'

CHAPTER FIFTEEN

THE SWEEP

Planning destruction for Don Joaquin, for Dave Kenny, and all who dared oppose him, Manfred von Wohl's eyes glowed with a bloody hue. His bristling mustache twitched. He drank deep from the bottle, and rose.

'I'll see you, then, Froleiks, around noon tomorrow,' he said.

'*Adios*,' said the sheriff. 'I'll be there with Dinny's bunch.'

Von Wohl went out, crossing the plaza toward the hotel. Several armed men who were always at his side, trailed after him.

Froleiks was whistling to himself, cheerily. He had thrown in his lot with the vicious von Wohl, hoping to make his fortune by following the Prussian's banner, and the prospect looked good to him. He finished off the inch or so of whisky left and tossed the bottle into a corner. He checked his Colt, and dropped a handful of carbine shells into a pocket. Then he turned down the lamp and blew out the flame.

Stepping out, Froleiks closed the door and snapped the padlock on it. As he stepped from the low stoop to the earth, the Rio Kid and Mireles hit him, a wiry hand choking off his startled cry.

136

It was a masterpiece of scouting, the way the Rio Kid, Walker and Mireles snaked Froleiks out of Soledad, half-dragging, half-carrying the panic-stricken renegade lawman whose eyes gleamed as he rolled them in his fright. A tight gag kept him from speaking, and his hands were fastened behind him.

Von Wohl men were coming back, after a fruitless hunt for the Rio Kid in the night. Other von Wohl gunnies were sifting through the settlement.

But avoiding them all the Rio Kid and his aides fetched their prisoner to the spot where Kenny and Carmody held the horses, in an open shed behind a darkened house. They tied the sheriff in front of the Rio Kid's saddle, and headed out. Celestino went first, checking the route out of the town.

'Won't von Wohl miss the skunk?' asked Carmody, when they were well away.

'I don't figger so,' said the Rio Kid. 'Von Wohl told him to hook over to a place called Dinny's Roost, to pick up more killers. Froleiks is supposed to meet von Wohl at the hacienda.'

The Rio Kid had Froleiks, and he was praying, inwardly, that the Castros would be able to rouse Guiterrez and get the main crew of fighting vaqueros to him in time. He hoped to reach the former Guiterrez rancho before von Wohl's main force returned.

'If not, I'll have to try and ambush 'em

137

later,' he thought.

It was late now, and he had to arrive before dawn. Besides, when he was miles out of Soledad, it was necessary to pause so he could work on Froleiks. He chose a clearing at the side of the road and, getting down, pulled the lawman off Saber and tore off the gag.

'Yuh ain't goin' to kill me, are yuh?' whined Froleiks. He was slobbering with fear.

The men all lighted cigarettes, and Froleiks could make out the grim faces in the ruby glows. They squatted in a circle about him, staring at him as he lay cowering on the ground.

At a nod from the Rio Kid, Celestino drew his long, shining knife, and bent over the sheriff, who gave a squeak of terror and shrank from the point at his throat.

'Eef you fight, I geeve you thees,' threatened Mireles.

It did not take too much acting to scare Froleiks to a pulp. He begged for mercy.

'One chance yuh got to live, Froleiks,' growled the Rio Kid ferociously. 'That is, help us down von Wohl. If yuh obey my orders, I'll see to it yuh ain't killed.'

'I—I'll do anything yuh want!' Froleiks was snatching straws as he found himself in the power of the Rio Kid.

*   *   *

The first von Wohl sentry challenged, at the spot where the lane turned in to the former Guiterrez hacienda.

'Halt!'

'Take it easy,' called Froleiks. 'It's me, feller, Sheriff Froleiks. The boss sent me on ahead. Who's in?'

'Hans is home, and ten or twelve of the boys—that's all. Most of 'em are snorin'—who's that—some of yore men?'

'Yeah,' said Froleiks, and called, 'Come on, fellers.'

He struck a match to light a cigar, as the Rio Kid had told him to do, after he had softened up the law officer for the job he needed done. Rapidly the Rio Kid came up, his head down, the rider dark in the night. The sentinel's eyes were temporarily dazzled by the glowing match in Froleiks' hand. What happened then, happened fast.

'*Bueno*, Froleiks,' growled the Rio Kid, after they had the first man disposed of. 'Get goin' and we'll work in to the house.'

He clapped his hands. Mireles, Dave Kenny, Walker and Carmody hurried up, and Froleiks moved on to contact the next guard. Froleiks was doublecrossing von Wohl in his avid desire to save his own life.

They snaffled two more sentries, and became aware that there was a faint lightening in the east, the false dawn. Froleiks was at the hacienda gate. He dismounted, and as he chatted with the armed retainer there, the Rio Kid and Mireles brought the man down with scarcely a sound.

Inside, the hacienda was quiet. Von Wohl had set up his headquarters here, at Don Joaquin's old homestead. It was larger, and more elaborately furnished than the Castro place.

'Don't let anybody snake through, boys,' ordered the Rio Kid.

Carmody remained at the front gate, from which vantage point he would trap anyone trying to run out that way. Dave Kenny, who had known the hacienda as home, padded swiftly across the patio to watch the rear exit.

Walker and Celestino went in with the Rio Kid. They saw Hans' huge form sprawled on a sofa in the great parlor. Other sleepers were lying on blanket beds in the room.

Froleiks swallowed in nervous fright, as the Rio Kid and Mireles tiptoed toward Hans. Jo Walker, gun in hand, stood ready at the entry. The invaders of the hacienda swept up what guns they saw.

A bearded killer muttered in his sleep, and turned over. Suddenly Hans awoke. The huge German sat bolt upright. There was a lamp burning on a nearby table. It had been turned down, but gave enough light to see by, and Hans saw everything instantly.

In spite of his size, Hans was fast. He had a shotgun close at hand, and without a word of warning he seized it, rolling to the floor. The Rio Kid was swinging, to fire, but Hans was quick.

Mireles moved with a tigerish lunge. The knife flashed in his slim brown hand, whipped straight through the air, and cut in under Hans' right arm, driving an inch through the fat. It threw Hans off balance. He roared with the shotgun, which tore a gaping hole in the mat and spattered buck into the air.

Celestino and the Rio Kid fired, Colts snarling almost at the same instant. Hans staggered. His arms went down, and a dazed glare came into his eyes.

'*Herr* von Wohl!' he screamed.

The great body lost its drive, and Hans crumpled to the mat.

The booming guns woke the rest.

'Watch out, Rio Kid!' trumpeted Jo Walker.

His carbine snapped, and a gunny gave a screech of pain, clutching at his punctured shoulder. Mireles and the Rio Kid turned on them. Mireles snatched up the shotgun, cocking the second trigger.

'Hold or I fire!' he shouted.

Hands went up, as the fight left the crew on guard. A shout and gunshot came from the patio, as Carmody checked a von Wohl man seeking escape. Kenny was busy, too.

When the sun rose over the Salinas country, the Rio Kid and his men were in possession of the rancho.

With their prisoners held in the storerooms, they made themselves at home, cooking breakfast and resting. But the Rio Kid watched constantly.

'I hope Guiterrez makes it, before von Wohl shows,' he kept saying.

It was a toss-up. The Castros would make a fast ride of it, but it would be necessary to collect the vaqueros and bring them across country to the hacienda.

Searching von Wohl's papers, locked in a steel box in his new office—the lid had been pried off in the blacksmith shop—the Rio Kid found fresh forgeries that had been begun by von Wohl. They were claims and notes against Guiterrez, Dave Kenny, the Castros and others who had settled on the tableland. Von Wohl was making ready to seize the coveted plateau so he could hold up Leland Stanford, and gain full control of the Salinas.

*   *   *

Hour after hour passed, the sun climbing high in the sky. Eyes burning from lack of sleep, Mireles, Pryor and the rest who held von Wohl's place kept watching, watching for signs of approaching friends or enemies.

'Dust on ze road!' Celestino sang out, at last.

'Who is it,' asked Jo Walker, 'von Wohl or the vaqueros?'

'Be ready to make the hosses, in case it's

von Wohl,' ordered the Rio Kid. 'We can't hold that mob off in a big place like this.'

It was anxious waiting, as they peered from the front windows of the hacienda, between the bars there in the outer wall. To the rear, Kenny had the saddled horses hidden by the bulk of the buildings.

A rider turned into the lane from the highway, sped toward them. Mireles gave a cheer.

'Ees Don Joaquin!'

Guiterrez, followed by his vaqueros, the Castros, the Estradas, Gascas, and other Californios summoned by the Rio Kid, galloped to the hacienda. They were well-armed, with guns, lassos, and knives.

Don Joaquin's white teeth gleamed as he waved to the Rio Kid and Mireles, waiting for him outside the patio gate. He had brought thirty fighting men along,, and the Rio Kid hastily called them in, placing their mounts in the stables.

They had hardly settled down when Dave Kenny, watching the road, announced the approach of another party.

It was Manfred von Wohl and his two-score men, coming home.

Crouched inside, at a vantage point, the Rio Kid peered out. As von Wohl came into the lane the Prussian spurred his gray mustang ahead, impatient to reach his quarters. He threw himself off his horse, and strode in the gate, spurs tinkling.

'Hans!' he called. 'Hans!'

The patio was deserted and von Wohl swore testily. His face was purple, from the exercise of riding and his burning anger which had not abated since the Rio Kid had bested him in Soledad.

'Hans, you fat rascal!' he roared. 'Where are you—where's everybody?'

He turned and went inside. Bunches of his men were dismounting, dropping their reins and coming through the gate.

As von Wohl entered the big parlor, the Rio Kid stepped out to greet him.

'Welcome home, von Wohl!'

Von Wohl froze in the doorway. His bulging eyes flicked to the carcass of the huge Hans, lying dead on the sofa where the Rio Kid had placed him, for all to see.

'Rio Kid!' gasped von Wohl, stupidly. He could not believe what he saw. Hans dead, his enemies in control. The guns of the Rio Kid surrounding him.

'You're cooked, von Wohl,' said the Rio Kid coldly. 'Reach, and step in here where we can take yore guns. Marshal Carmody's goin' to run yuh to Sacramento. We got a dozen charges agin yuh—killin's, forgeries—'

The Rio Kid had not drawn. His Colts reposed in their oiled, supple holsters. Von Wohl, desperate in the moment of defeat, threw himself back with a sharp cry, and fell, scrambling around the doorsill. Leaping to his feet, the Prussian raced for the patio, screaming for his men.

The Rio Kid and Guiterrez were after him instantly. They could see the sunlit enclosure through the wide door. It was filled with churning gunnies. Shots burst in the warm air, and cries of terror. Lining the roofs and walls covering the patio were the Salinas folks, commanded by Celestino, Walker, Carmody and other lieutenants. Their guns held the gathering, and the gate had slammed shut from outside.

Expert ropers, vaqueros of the range, made their casts, looping those who tried to put up a fight. Guns went off in the air or into the ground, and the mob milled in mad confusion.

Von Wohl slid to a stop, seeing the debacle of his forces. He turned, a mad beast at bay, whipped up his Colt to fire into his arch-enemy, the Rio Kid. The Prussian killer's blue eyes bulged like twin blue marbles. His nostrils were dilated, his mustache twitched, the points bristling.

'You will die, Rio Kid!' he screamed.

His pistol roared, reverberating in the arched hallway. The Rio Kid, down on one knee, fired. He felt the burn of von Wohl's slug on his left arm, and his Colt kicked in his right hand.

Von Wohl was hit. He leaned against the adobe wall, his head drooping, the fight gone from his body. Free guns had won the battle, and the vicious von Wohl slowly slumped to the stone flags of the passageway.

*   *   *

Behind them, the Rio Kid and Celestino Mireles had left the Salinas land freed of von Wohl's tyranny. The Prussian was dead, his henchmen were under arrest, and Marshal Ben Carmody would see to the law's honors, the conviction of Froleiks and the gunmen.

Guiterrez had recovered his rancho, and the Californios held the fertile new plateau, with its boundless water table.

The Rio Kid and his trail-mate had dropped old Jo Walker, their comrade in the struggle, at his nephew's, and after a rest, had ridden on, for the wild trails called the Rio Kid and his partner.

'Nice folks, those kinfolks friends of yores, Celestino,' said the Rio Kid. 'Salt of the earth.'

'*Si, si*. Good people,' Mireles nodded.

Dave Kenny had his Teresa, and his farm. He would make his life among the Californios, whom he loved and admired.

'Let's hope other folks appreciate 'em, too,' said the Rio Kid, 'and that they all live in peace!'

The Rio Kid, on the supple dun, turned his eyes ahead. There were other fights to be made, and the dangerous life beckoned.

We hope you have enjoyed this Large Print book. Other Chivers Press or Thorndike Press Large Print books are available at your library or directly from the publishers.

For more information about current and forthcoming titles, please call or write, without obligation, to:

Chivers Large Print
published by BBC Audiobooks Ltd
St James House, The Square
Lower Bristol Road
Bath BA2 3BH
UK
email: bbcaudiobooks@bbc.co.uk
www.bbcaudiobooks.co.uk

OR

Thorndike Press
295 Kennedy Memorial Drive
Waterville
Maine 04901
USA
www.gale.com/thorndike
www.gale.com/wheeler

All our Large Print titles are designed for easy reading, and all our books are made to last.